Nelle

Emma Charles

Paperback edition: August 2025
ISBN 979-8-9997434-0-4 (paperback)
ISBN 979-8-9997434-1-1 (ebook)

www.emmacharles.net

To Marsha,
Big sister extraordinaire

CHAPTER ONE
Brushy Fork, Lawrence County, Kentucky
1939

Water ran cold and clear over the flat rounded stones that made up the bed of Brushy Fork. Twelve-year-old Pheen wriggled her toes in the water, sighed with contentment, bent and picked up a flat rock from beneath the surface of the water to watch a crawdad scuttle away.

"Josephine Joy, hurry up!" Nelle, a few feet farther down the creek, demanded. Pheen dropped the rock and hurried to catch up with her sister, Elanor 'Nelle' Rose. At thirteen—almost fourteen, for she had a birthday coming up in the next week, her older sister was a good head taller and sturdier built than Pheen. Her hair was as blonde as all the other Keller cousins they shared. Only Pheen, with her chestnut waves and skinny knees, stood out amongst them.

The dirt lane wound along the creek's path, with a screen of trees and brush hiding the creek from view. The girls were now out of sight of the farmhouse once they'd left the bottom behind where their momma kept her kitchen garden. Nelle had reached the fence which came down the hillside and crossed the creek. The water pooled deeper under the fence, making it easy to duck under the lowest strand of wire to reach the pasture beyond. Pheen followed her sister under the fence, hesitating once she was on the other side.

"Come on!" Nelle exhorted. She stood shin-deep in the water, hands on hips, and shook her head. "Will you come on, Josephine Joy Keller? Daddy's old bull is up yonder in the woods. He won't come chasing us down here!" Splashing, Pheen ran down the creek bed to where a second fence crossed the stream, enclosing the pasture where their father, John H. Keller, kept his prize bull Devil during the summer. Before the weather turned cold, he'd have Devil in a sturdy stall in the barn, but for now he was free to roam the hillside pasture.

Pheen could hear splashing up ahead. As the creek curved away from the road, it widened into a pool deep enough for swimming. This far into summer, someone could always be counted on to make use of the swimming hole. When chores were done or one could sneak away— as she and Nelle were doing, they'd usually find someone else enjoying the cold water, the tire swing hung from a branch of a tree on the far bank, and the flat rocks one could stretch out on to dry off. They'd all been swimming since they were no bigger than tadpoles themselves, so the grown-ups didn't worry about anyone drowning.

"Whoo-eee!" Pheen watched as her older brother George cannonballed off a rock into the deepest part of the pool.

"Stop showing off, George Keller!" Nelle jeered. Her brother flipped a streak of water at his sister, who ducked. Nelle was older than George by a year and almost two years' older than Pheen. Lizzie and Mae Arnett squealed as George splashed them as he swam back to the bank. The girls lived up the holler where the creek branched off. Pheen knew without looking that their older brother, Hobart, would be close by. Those girls weren't allowed out of the yard without him. He was two years older than Lizzie, who was the same age as Nelle.

Her sister, she saw, was swimming out into the middle of the swimming hole when Hobart rose out of the water behind her and dunked Nelle until she came up sputtering and yelling.

"You just wait, Hobart! I'll get even with you!"

Pheen made for the bank nearest the tire swing. Mae ran around the edge of the swimming hole to join her.

"I'll push you, Pheen. We can take turns swinging."

As Pheen swung out over the creek, she heard Lizzie shrieking as George grabbed her by a foot and threatened to pull her into the swimming hole.

"C'mon, Lizzie, you gotta get wet when you go swimming!"

"George Keller, my daddy'll skin you alive if I come home all wet!"

Fat chance, Pheen thought. Lizzie couldn't swim for a lick and they all knew it. Mostly she came to keep an eye on her older brother. Pheen didn't like the way he looked at Nelle when he thought no one could see him. And Lizzie didn't like it one bit either, Pheen could tell. She might come down to the swimming hole with Hobart and Mae, she might even enjoy George's attention, but those Arnetts were all a bit stuck on themselves.

The tire swung Pheen back to the creek bank and she jumped off so Mae could have a turn. Mae had black hair straight as a stick that hung down to her shoulders, and she was scrawny as a molting hen, nothing like the plumpness and careful brown curls of her older sister. But Mae had a sweeter disposition. Pheen reckoned it was living with her sister that did it. A girl could be bitter at being second or she could just be glad not to be Lizzie. Pheen gave the tire an extra hard push and sent Mae hollering out over the swimming hole. Mae jumped off as the swing reached its highest point above the water and somersaulted into the swimming hole. Water sprayed

Lizzie and George, who hooted with laughter and dove into the creek. He swam out to Mae, clapping her on the shoulder. Lizzie scooted back from the water's edge, stood up, and stalked off.

Pheen's eyes narrowed. Where was Nelle? And where was Hobart? Her glance swept the edges of the swimming hole, and then she spied them, sitting on a rock apart from the others, heads close together, bent over something she couldn't make out. Hobart had his arm around Nelle's shoulders, drawing her closer. Suddenly, George and Mae popped up on either side of the rock where Hobart and Nelle sat, throwing great armfuls of water over the two from either side. Nelle scrambled to her feet, laughing and wiping the water from her eyes. Hobart jumped up, his face red, his dark blond hair dripping, and shook his fist at George.

"One of these days, George Keller, I'll beat the tar out of you!"

Then Lizzie was there, pulling at her brother's arm, turning him away from the creek.

"C'mon, Hobart!" She threw a spiteful look at her sister. "You get out of that water right now, Mae Arnett! We are going home."

Pheen, Nelle, and George were coming through the kitchen garden in the bottom near the creek when their Grandma Lavinia spied them.

"You three better get in the house and get some dry clothes on before your momma or daddy sees you. Sneaking off in the middle of the day! I swear, what was you three thinking?"

"Thinking we'd go swimming and cool off," George laughed and swiped a wet smooch on his grandmother's cheek as he ducked around her.

"You picking greens for supper?" Nelle asked. "I'll finish for you, Grandma. You go on up to the porch and get out of this heat." She took the basket from her grandmother and nodded at Pheen. "Go on, help Grandma up the bank. I'll be there in a minute."

Her grandmother pulled a hankie from her apron pocket and wiped her forehead.

"Come help me, Pheen, I believe I'll sit a spell on the porch. You go on in the house and help your momma."

Pheen saw her grandmother settled with a sigh in a large wicker rocker.

"I'll be right back, Grandma. I'll bring you a glass of cold water."

Her mother took one look at the clothes, now mostly dry, on her second daughter and smiled. "Have a fun time at the swimming hole?"

Pheen took a glass from the cupboard and poured cold water into it.

"We did until George and Mae splashed Nelle and Hobart. That Hobart threw a fit and Lizzie made Mae get out of the water and go home."

Her mother raised an eyebrow, but made no comment except to remind Pheen. "The oven's hot if you want to make a pone of cornbread when you come back in. I've got beans cooking, there's a big plate of tomatoes sliced on the counter, and there'll be a wilted salad to go with our supper."

"Nelle's bringing the greens in, Momma," she called over her shoulder as she left the kitchen, pausing as

Virgie and Lewis, her younger sister and brother, came running into the kitchen.

"Mama," Virgie pouted, "Lewis threw a rock at me."

"I never did!" Lewis shouted. "I was aiming at that ole gander and you know it, Virgie!"

The younger girl stamped her foot, her blonde curls bouncing about her face.

"My name is not Virgie, Lewis Keller. I've told you a million times. It's Virginia!"

Their mother sighed and shook her apron skirt at her two youngest. "You two get out of my kitchen with your fussing. You can set the table, Miss Virginia Keller. And you, Lewis, go find your papa and help him finish his chores."

"But I'm tired, Mama!" Pheen didn't wait to hear any more of Virgie's whining. She grabbed the glass of water for her grandmother and passed Nelle coming in from the front porch with the basket of fresh greens.

"Nelle," Virgie cried as she caught sight of her oldest sister through the dining room doorway. "Nelle, it's not fair! Momma's making me set the table by myself!"

Pheen's eyes widened as she heard Nelle respond to their younger sister.

"You're big enough to help Momma, Virgie. You're all of eight years old now!"

"It's not fair, Nelle! I don't want to set the table!" Virgie's voice was rising, on the verge of tears. "It's not fair!"

Grandma Lavinia accepted the glass of cold water from Pheen, drank it down, and sat back in the rocker with a sigh.

"It sure makes it easier to have you girls helping your momma around the place." She shook her head.

"And that includes Virgie. She's getting too old to be a crybaby any time she has to do a lick of work."

Pheen indicated the door with a jerk of her shoulder.

"You know Nelle usually spoils her, Grandma. She turns on the tears and Nelle lets her get away with anything." She grinned. "I bet her eyes about popped out of her head just now!"

Dinner was over early, and Pheen ran a sink full of hot sudsy water to wash the dishes. Usually she and Nelle worked together to clean up the kitchen, giving their mother a chance to take care of her lovebirds or play the piano for a piece while their daddy relaxed on the couch in the living room and read the *Big Sandy* newspaper or listened to the radio. Grandma Lavinia sat in the old rocker and took up her bible to read before bed.

But this night, Nelle turned to Virgie.

"Virgie, you hop over here and dry these dishes." She put up a hand as Virgie opened her mouth to protest. "I don't want a word out of you or I'll make you sleep with Pheen tonight."

Pheen looked at her older sister, amazed. "She's not sleeping with me," she declared.

Nelle turned away from Virgie and winked at Pheen.

"Daddy's brought me some fabric from the store at Blaine today. For my birthday next week." Her eyes lit up. "You know that ad for the clothing store in the *Big Sandy* from last Wednesday?" At Pheen's nod, she continued. "I'm going to make a pattern for that skirt and jacket we liked so much!"

With Nelle's attention diverted from her for a moment, Virgie headed for the dining room door.

"Not so fast, young lady!" Nelle called, reached out, and caught her by the shoulder. "You march right over there and help Pheen." Virgie's mouth drew down and her eyes filled with tears. "I mean it," Nelle's voice was stern. "It won't take long at all, Virgie. And," she added, "Pheen will help you. Look, she's almost got the washing done while you're standing there pouting."

Pheen shot her sister a look, but didn't say anything. She'd end up drying most of those dishes herself, she knew. But that was okay. Nelle was the best seamstress on Brushy, if not the whole of Lawrence County, Kentucky, Pheen thought with pride. And Nelle was generous, sharing her hand-me-downs with Pheen and taking them in as needed to make sure everything fit just right. When Nelle finished that new suit, there wasn't a soul who would be able to tell it hadn't been bought from the store or ordered from a catalogue ready-made.

CHAPTER TWO

Sitting on the porch swing, Pheen stretched out her long legs and curled and uncurled her toes as she pushed the swing to and fro. George looked up from the porch floor where he lay sprawled, engrossed in his Superman comic.

"Wow, Pheen! This character Leonard Trent's a real wise guy. Superman's gonna crack his head like an egg!" He chuckled.

"When you're done, I want to read it," she reminded him, knowing full well that her brother would take his time reading the comic through, then would reread it until he'd memorized every word before she'd ever get her hands on it.

Lewis came bounding up the steps, his bare feet muddy, his red-tick hound Ruby at his heels. The old dog shook herself and George leapt up with his precious comic.

"Hey, Lewis! Watch it!"

Lewis grabbed for the comic, but George held it out of reach.

"Go on, get that mangy dog out of here! And you better wash your feet off at the pump before you go on in the house!"

His younger brother gave a great huff, then laughed and jumped off the porch. Ruby heaved a big sigh and trotted down the steps after the boy.

"Pheen!"

Pheen could hear Nelle clattering halfway down the stairs, leaning over the banister to holler again.

"Josephine Joy! Come up here and help me, will you?"

"Here, slip this on, then stand up on that chair," Nelle ordered when Pheen had followed her sister up to the bedroom they shared with Virgie at the head of the stairs. Their grandmother's Singer sewing machine stood in front of the window which overlooked the front porch, giving the older girl plenty of light for her sewing. Nelle's cat, a big yellow and white tomcat, lay on the bed, watching the goings-on. Once Pheen was in place, Nelle stood before her with her adjustable sewing gauge in one hand and a pin-stuffed cushion in the other hand.

"I just need to get this hem pinned and sewn and the skirt will be finished." She turned a critical eye on her handiwork. "Turn around slow first, so I can see how those pleats fall."

Pheen did as ordered, smoothing the fabric down.

"It's gorgeous, Nelle!" She looked down over her shoulder at her older sister, now kneeling as she turned the tweed fabric up for the hem. "I mean it. I'm not just saying that because you're my sister." She sighed. "You'll be the best-dressed girl in the high school when school starts!" She grinned as Nelle finished pinning and steadied her younger sister as Pheen stepped down from the chair and slipped off the skirt. "That ole Lizzie Arnett is gonna be green with envy when she sees you in this suit!"

"It's not Lizzie I want to see me in this suit," Nelle retorted. Pheen's eyebrows rose in astonishment.

"Then who you making it for, Elanor Rose Keller?"

Nelle shrugged and turned away.

"That's for me to know and you to find out, Miss Nosey-Parker!"

As Pheen gave her sister a sharp glance, Nelle scooped up the extra fabric on the bed and shook it out.

"Look here, Pheen," she nodded at the bed where newsprint was scotch-taped into a pattern. "Daddy got so much fabric, there's enough left to make a second skirt." She picked up the newspaper advertisement with the young women's fashions. "See this one here? I've made a pattern for it, too. And I can cut the fronts for a vest from the scraps of this tweed fabric. If I use some plain fabric for the back, then you'll have a new suit of your own for school."

She smiled at the look of surprise and delight on Pheen's face.

"Can't have my little sister starting high school in hand-me-downs!" She grinned at Pheen. "We'll be the two best-dressed girls in high school!"

At Pheen's frown, Nelle squeezed her sister's shoulders.

"Don't be scared, Pheen!"

Pheen tried to smile, gulped.

"School's starting so soon now! What if I'm not smart enough? What if those town kids make fun of me?" She sat down on the bed, all her earlier excitement deflated.

"You listen to me, Josephine Joy Keller! Miss Hillis wouldn't send you on to high school, if she didn't think you could do the work." She shoved her fabric and patterns out of the way and sat down on the edge of the bed by her sister. "Listen, you might be a little younger than some of the kids, but you're smart as a whip and you know it!" She hugged Pheen again. "Besides, you think Daddy and Momma would let you go if they didn't believe you could hold your own with them town kids?"

Nelle's cat stood, stretched, and head-butted Pheen's arm. She gathered the cat up and hid her face in its fur. Nelle reached for the skirt pattern and the extra fabric.

"I'll cut your skirt out, if you'll help Momma with supper later." She gave her sister a wide grin. "And if any of those uppity town girls gives you any trouble, Pheen, they'll have to answer to me!"

Supper over, Pheen sat scrunched up at one end of the couch, engrossed in her book, *The Good Earth*. Miss Hillis had suggested she read it over the summer. Nelle sat with her legs draped over the armchair next to Pheen, idly turning the pages of the newest *Photoplay* magazine and blowing and popping a large bubble with her bubblegum every few minutes.

"Elanor Rose, you don't stop with that bubblegum, I'm gonna make you spit it out."

"Aw, Daddy! Don't be such a grouch!"

"I mean it. I'm trying to listen to the news."

John Keller sat at the other end of the couch, next to the radio. He leaned over to fiddle with the dial. Radio reception tonight was staticky, with a storm brewing beyond the hills.

"Rain's coming," Grandma Lavinia remarked, looking up from her bible, her rocking chair stilled for a moment.

"War's coming!" George said. He was sprawled on the floor beneath the radio, as intent on the news as his father.

"Hush that kind of talk!" Pheen looked up from her book. Her mother was just coming downstairs from getting Virgie and Lewis to bed. She sank down on the couch next to her husband. He put an arm around her shoulders and pulled her close to him.

"No need to worry yet, Nan." He prodded George with his foot. "President Roosevelt's declared that America's neutral. We ain't gonna be fighting in no war."

George rolled away out of reach of his father and sat up.

"Well, that's not what Mr. Thompson said after church last Sunday." He scooted farther away from the radio. "Maybe it won't start until I'm old enough to fight!"

"You know I respect Walker Thompson, he's a good man," his father nodded at his son. "A man's entitled to his opinion, but I think he's wrong." He leaned forward and shook his finger at George. "And you're not going anywhere, young man. When you're done with school, I need you to help me with the timber and the lumber mill." He turned the radio dial until the dulcet tones of Dinah Shore crooning came on and pulled Nan closer. Pheen relaxed. If her daddy said there wasn't going to be a war, then George had better keep his thoughts to himself. Her brother threw her a look she knew all too well. He was as stubborn as their daddy.

The front porch floor was cool in the morning, the sun not yet high enough to warm up the valley. Pheen and George sat shoulder to shoulder at the steps. Pheen scratched Ruby's ears. The old hound stirred sleepily and gave a lick at Pheen's hand.

"I mean it, Pheen," George kept his voice low, half-an eye turned to the front door. They could hear the grown-ups still talking over breakfast in the dining room and the clatter of plates. "Canada's done declared war on

Germany. You know I look older than I am. Why, I could pass for seventeen right now."

Pheen put a hand on her brother's arm. "You mean you'd try to join the army up in Canada?" George nodded.

"Sh-h!" he cautioned as Pheen gasped. "Not so loud. Anyways, I'm not going anywhere yet. But if the war don't end soon, you bet I'm gonna fight them Germans!" He stood up as their father came out into the side yard, calling for him. "I gotta go help Daddy, don't you say a word to nobody!"

"I won't," she promised, but her thoughts were bleak. Somehow, George's words made the war in Europe all the more real to her. If George felt that way, what about the other young men she knew? What about their cousins Frank and Harry, both grown and just out of school? And what if George and Mr. Thompson were right and their daddy was wrong? She'd heard old Mr. O'Bryant at the store in Blaine talking to other customers the last time she'd gone to the store with her mother. He seemed mighty worried.

She started as Nelle dropped down beside her.

"What's got you looking so serious this morning?"

"All this talk of war, Nelle. What do you think? You think any of our boys will go off to war now that Canada's joined?" A thought occurred to her. "Like Hobart. He's what, seventeen? Almost eighteen now?"

Nelle snorted. "Hobart's seventeen, but he's not going anywhere, if I have anything to say about it. You can get that notion out of your head right now." She jumped up before Pheen could answer. "Come on, Momma's going to can corn today and she needs us to get the laundry done for her."

Pheen watched her sister stalk into the house, letting the screen door bang behind her. What on earth, she wondered, made Nelle so sure that Hobart wouldn't go off to fight, given the chance? He sure didn't mind picking fights with their own brother, for one thing. Plus, it would give him bragging rights, that is, if he lived to come home again. Nelle sure was touchy this morning, she hoped she'd get in a better temper while they got the laundry done. Pheen stood up and followed her sister inside. Maybe, she thought, Grandma Lavinia would help with the laundry and she could cut corn off the cob for their mother.

Lying in bed across from the one Nelle shared with Virgie, Pheen whispered, "You awake, Nelle?"

"Mmm," came her sister's low voice. "What? Don't wake up Virgie, you know she takes forever to get back to sleep."

"Why're you so sure Hobart wouldn't go off to war? Do you think Frank or Harry might? I'm scared of all this talk about war."

A long moment of silence answered her.

"We aren't at war, Pheen. Don't be a goose, okay? Nobody's going off to fight. Now, go to sleep."

Turning on her side away from her sisters' bed, Pheen reflected on Nelle's answer. Her older sister was always so sure about things. But that didn't stop Pheen from worrying, and, she reflected before sleep claimed her, Nelle hadn't really answered her questions.

CHAPTER THREE

John Keller sat at the dining table, counting out dollar bills from a tin box. When he finished smoothing out every crumpled bill, he handed a portion of the money to his wife.

"Here you go, Nan." He grinned at her across the table. "The timber sales came in a little higher than expected. This here," he pointed at the money he'd given her, "oughta be enough for a new dress each for the girls, some new overalls for the boys, and school shoes for them all."

Nan reached across the table to grip his hand in hers. "Don't think I don't appreciate how hard you work for us, John!"

Nelle, who'd been peeking around the dining room door with Pheen, whooped and ran to her father, throwing her arms around his neck.

"Thank you, Daddy!"

Pheen put an arm around his shoulders and hugged him.

"You're the best, Daddy!"

Virgie sidled up to her mother. "Is all that for me?" Her voice wheedling, she turned a big smile on her father. "There's lots of pretty dresses at the store in Louisa!"

"Nope, Virgie! There's enough there for ever'body." He pointed at his wife. "And that includes you, Nan. You pick out something special just for yourself." He waggled a finger at her as she started to protest. "I mean it, young lady!"

Pheen giggled. "Nelle and I'll make sure she does, Daddy!"

He put his arm around her. "That's my girls! I was thinking I could drive you'uns up to town before dinner today." He fanned the bills in his hand. "And we'll treat ourselves to hamburgers and sodas after your shopping's all done."

Nelle grabbed Pheen. "Come on! Let's round up George and Lewis!"

Nan came around the table to give her husband a hug and plant a kiss on the top of his head. "I'll see if Lavinia is awake. She was feeling poorly earlier."

The dressing room at the back of the dry goods store was stuffy, and Pheen lifted the hair off the back of her neck as she looked at herself in the mirror. Instead of a dress, she'd found a tailored sky blue blouse and a long-sleeved russet sweater with contrast piping at the neck and sleeves, both of which would look great with the tweed skirt Nelle had made for her. She held up one, then the other against her torso. If she mixed these with pieces she already owned, she'd have a bunch of new outfits for school, she thought. The door rattled.

"C'mon, hurry up, Pheen!" Nelle called. "Wait till you see the dress I've found!"

Folding up the blouse and sweater, Pheen opened the door for her sister. A dress with a dark blue velvet skirt and a coppery satin top preceded her sister into the dressing room. Nelle's eyes sparkled as she thrust the dress at Pheen. "Here, hold this while I get undressed."

Pheen undid the buttons down the bodice of the dress. It had short, slightly puffed sleeves, a Peter Pan collar trimmed with a narrow ruffle, and a fitted peplum waist. The A-line skirt hugged Nelle's curves as she settled the dress over her hips and did up the buttons. As

Nelle pirouetted before the mirror, Pheen's eyes widened as she caught sight of the price tag.

"You girls about ready?" Their mother called after a knock at the door. "Your daddy's waiting to take us out to eat!"

"It's the most beautiful dress I've ever seen! But Nelle," Pheen sighed, "look at the price! And you couldn't wear it for school days!"

Nelle finished dressing and turned the dress around so her sister could see the side seam.

"Look here, some big old gal's tried this on and busted the seam out good." She folded up the dress and turned the price tag over to reveal a second price. "I found this on the sale rack. You know I can fix the damage easy."

Nelle looked in the dressing room mirror and gave one final pat to her hair.

"I don't plan to wear this just anywhere, Miss Josephine Joy! It's for dancing!" She opened the door before Pheen could say what was on her mind. Just who did Nelle think she would be going dancing with?

Nelle and George slid into either side of a booth at the Dixie Diner, making room for Pheen. Their parents and Grandma Lavinia sat at a table adjacent to the booth. When Virgie tried to squeeze in next to Nelle, she pushed her youngest sister away.

"Go on, baby," she told her. "You sit with Momma. Not with us!"

Virgie flounced away. Their grandma pulled out a chair for the girl.

"You sit right here between me and Lewis, honey. Your daddy's going to order us some hamburgers and maybe a milkshake each." She winked at her son.

The diner was packed. The Kellers, Pheen noted, weren't the only family finishing up school shopping with dinner out. A waitress stopped at their parents' table and took drink orders—coffee for the grown-ups and sodas for Lewis and Virgie.

"Root beer, please," she heard Lewis pipe up. John Keller nodded at his older children.

"Them three are with us," he told the waitress. "Hamburgers and French fries for everybody, unless," he looked to his mother. "Would you rather have the special?"

"That's roast beef, gravy, two vegetables, your choice of dessert, and your beverage for fifty cents," the waitress elaborated.

"Thank you, John, but I'll have a hamburger, too. With mustard and ketchup and pickles," she ordered. "But I wouldn't mind a piece of that coconut cream pie I saw in the case for dessert."

"That'll be fine, Mama. I reckon we're all going to have us some dessert. I don't think anybody here'd say no to ice cream?"

Lewis grinned at his daddy. "Not if it's strawberry!"

Pheen and George ordered Cokes, while Nelle pursed her lips over the menu. "Coke for me, too," she decided at last and handed the menu to the waitress.

George half-rose in his seat and waved at someone across the room.

"Who you waving at?" Pheen asked, looking around.

"Mae and Lizzie Arnett are over there with Hobart, the other side of the room," he told her and laughed at

Nelle. "Hobart must've driven them into town, I don't see Mr. and Miz Arnett anywhere." He sighed. "Must be nice to have your license and a car to drive."

Mae waved when she saw them looking her way, but Lizzie poked her sister with a menu to get her attention.

"Look at all those packages! They must have bought half the shop this afternoon!" Pheen touched Nelle's arm. "They can buy all the clothes they want, but nothing they have there will hold a candle to what you've made!"

Their waitress brought their drinks.

"Your orders will be up in a few minutes," she told their father. "The kitchen's hopping tonight!"

Nelle took a long sip of her Coke, turning half-way round in her seat to face the dining room.

"That's right, Daddy," Pheen spoke up as she listened to her parents banter. "Nelle and I found the sweetest dress for Momma today. We'll make her try it on and show you when we get home." She poked her sister. "Won't we, Nelle?"

But Nelle wasn't paying attention to her family, her gaze was locked on the other side of the room, her mouth set in a straight line. As their waitress returned with baskets loaded with a burger and fries for each of them, Pheen twisted about enough to see Lizzie, Mae, and Hobart's table. Hobart was swiveled about in his chair, turned away from his sisters, talking and laughing with the girls in the booth next to his table.

"That looks like Helen Prater and those cousins of hers—Dolly and Lucille."

Nelle busied herself with reconstructing her burger, after plucking off the pickles.

"Hobart can talk to anybody he wants. I don't see why you think I'd care."

Taken aback, Pheen looked at George and didn't say a word.

They'd almost finished their burgers, when Howard and Junior Jones and Les Clark stopped by their booth.

Howard was tall, with brown hair, brown eyes, and an easy smile. His younger brother Junior was red-haired, freckled, with a grin that matched Howard's. Les was a shorter, stouter version of his friend Howard. They were the same ages as Nelle and George.

"Just stopped to say hello!" Howard smiled, fully aware that although John Keller's attention might be on his wife's conversation, the man would hear every word spoken to his daughters. "Looking forward to seeing you all in school next week!"

Pheen couldn't help but notice Howard was looking at her sister as he spoke. Junior poked George with his elbow.

"Bet we get ole Williams for history this year, huh, George?"

Pheen missed her brother's reply. She'd glanced across the restaurant in time to see Hobart's smile wiped off his flushed face as he watched Howard lean over to say something to Nelle.

CHAPTER FOUR

"Josephine, would you hold up a moment?" Pheen waited by Mr. Wheeler's desk as the rest of the class filed out. English class was the last period of her school day. It was also her favorite class.

The teacher sat at his desk and picked up a paper from a stack in front of him.

"This is your book report on *The Good Earth*, Josephine." He took his glasses off and tapped them against her report. "I just wanted to let you know that you did a fine job. Well-written. Better than some of my seniors could do, if I say so." He gave a little laugh. "You see Miss Hillis, you give her my regards. I trust her judgment, you're going to do well in high school, Josephine, if your work continues to be this good."

Pheen stammered her thanks and hurried from the room. George was loitering in the hallway outside the classroom.

"You in trouble already, Pheen?"

Seeing her red face, he gave her a quick hug.

"Where's Nelle? We don't want to miss the bus."

George shook his head. "Don't know. She must've gone outside already. Come on!"

Climbing aboard the rickety yellow school bus, Pheen scanned the bus for her sister, while George headed for a group of rowdy boys who always sat in the rear on the bus's bench seat. She found a seat by herself and fretted as she looked out the window. Where was Nelle? What if she missed the bus? It was five miles' walk home from where the bus dropped them off on Route 32 at the head of the dirt road that wound along Brushy Creek. How would her sister get home?

As the bus driver began to close the doors, a flustered Nelle ran laughing up the bus steps.

"Hold up, Mr. Hayes!" she cried. "You can't leave without me!"

The driver gave her a grin and shut the doors closed behind her.

"Next time, I jus' might, Nelle."

Nelle caught sight of Pheen and hurried down the aisle to flop onto the seat next to her sister.

"Whew!" She blew a big bubble, popped it, and laughed at the look on Pheen's face.

"Don't worry about me, little sister!" She shook Pheen's arm. "I was waiting by Mr. Wheeler's classroom, but you didn't come out. Then I went outside and before I know it, old Mr. Hayes was about to leave without me!" She laughed, then leaned across Pheen to wave at a passing car full of kids from school.

"Look at that Lucille!" Nelle shook her head and laughed again. "You'd think somebody would tell her that red lipstick ain't her color."

Pheen said nothing. It hadn't escaped her notice that Nelle hadn't said just what she'd been doing before the bus started to leave. And if she wasn't mistaken, that was Hobart driving the car that had passed the bus.

Their daddy was waiting at the bus stop for them in the farm truck. Pheen breathed a sigh of relief. That five-mile walk at the end of the school day was wearying.

"You girls climb up here in the cab with me," he called, leaning over to open the door for them. "'Fraid you'll have to ride in the back, George."

Supper had come and gone, the table cleared and the dishes washed, when Pheen sat down again at the table and pulled out her history book. George sat at the other end of the table, helping Lewis with his multiplication tables. Virgie sat next to Nelle, who was reading her English lesson for the next day. Virgie had a ruled sheet of paper before her and was concentrating, her tongue stuck out, as she wrote. She stopped and held the paper up for Nelle to see.

"Look at my A, Nelle." When Nelle didn't answer, she tugged at her older sister's arm. "Look how good I can write my As!"

"Very good, Virgie." Nelle gave the paper Virgie was flourishing a cursory look and returned to her English book. "Now let me be, I need to finish reading this."

Virgie held up her paper so Pheen could see it.

"Look here! Look how good I can make an A."

"Yes, you sure can, Virgie," Pheen replied. "Now keep going. Aren't you supposed to do a whole row of them for practice?"

Virgie's lower lip came out. ""I shouldn't have to! This one's perfect! That old Miss Hillis is so mean!"

"Hold still, will you?" Nelle sectioned off another strand of Pheen's hair, rolled it around her finger close to the scalp, then bobby-pinned it in place. "There! You'll have a head full of waves in the morning."

The sisters sat on the bed together, Virgie asleep in the other bed. Nelle had already pin-curled her own blonde waves, but insisted on doing Pheen's hair, too. From the living room downstairs, they could hear the radio tuned to Lowell Thomas' radio show and a stern voice.

"…German troops have crossed into France…."

"Now, Nan," their father's soothing voice floated up to them.

Nelle hopped off the bed.

"I'm going to shut that window. It gets too cold in here at night for me." On her way to the window, she shut the bedroom door and with it the sounds from downstairs. "I swear, you're as anxious as Momma. Say your prayers, Pheen. Now go to sleep. We got to be up a mite early in the morning." She hugged Pheen. "I'll do your hair for you."

Pheen slipped down under the covers as Nelle turned out the light and got into her own bed next to Virgie. Pheen's thoughts were as cold as the mid-October night. She could feel it in her bones, horrifying things were happening out there in the world beyond Brushy. What made Nelle so sure those events wouldn't touch them? She shut her eyes tight and clasped her hands together. Her prayers were longer that night and as she drifted off to sleep, it seemed to her that she could hear the faraway sounds of marching feet.

Standing at her locker, Pheen fumbled the combination on the lock. Nelle, as promised, had combed out her hair into soft waves this morning. She'd worn her blue blouse with the skirt and matching vest Nelle had sewn, and her saddle shoes looked brand-new still. Her confidence high, she'd not been nervous when Mr. Pritchard had called on her in algebra class, nor as she walked the halls between classes. But it was lunchtime now. She hated lunch period because none of her friends from the school on Brushy had been promoted to the high school. Every day she ate by herself.

The locker door swung open on her third try. She put her books away, pulling out her lunch bag and the novel *Anne of Avonlea* to keep her company as she ate. She and Nelle and George were given ten cents each day to get a bowl of soup and carton of milk to go with the sandwich and apple their mother packed for them. Pheen saw an empty table near the back of the lunchroom and set her tray down. Her sandwich was peanut butter with strawberry jam made from their own strawberries, on two thick slices of homemade bread. Grandma Lavinia still made all their bread. She set her sandwich aside and concentrated on her soup, aware of the lunchroom filling up.

"Oops!" Someone's elbow knocked her hard in the middle of her shoulders. As she looked around, Helen Prater smirked. "So sorry!" Then she turned back to her friends and they all giggled. Pheen felt her face reddening and took a deep breath, scooting her chair closer to her table.

"That's Elanor's little sister. You know, those girls live way out somewhere off 32, in a holler." Lucille's loud whisper carried clearly to Pheen.

A second voice piped up, that was Lizzie, spiteful.

"That Elanor, you wait and see if she doesn't find herself in trouble one day, chasing after the older boys."

"Thinks she's something hot," a third voice chimed in. Dolly, or maybe Helen, Pheen wasn't sure which. Both girls had a nasally voice. "And her sister thinks she's so smart. Teacher's pet!"

The whole table laughed.

Then a tray was plunked down at Pheen's table and the whispers stopped. It was Mae.

"You don't mind if I sit with you, do you, Pheen?" Mae was already pulling out a chair. "My classes got changed and my lunch period is the same as yours now."

Pheen was one of the first out of her English classroom at the end of the day. Students were streaming out of classrooms, loud, heading for lockers and buses, those who rode home. She spotted Nelle coming along, and her heart lit up with pride. Blonde waves framing her strong face, Nelle was laughing at something her friend was saying. Boys' heads turned as she passed by, as if a magnet pulled their attention to her. Her group of girlfriends swelled as other girls clustered about her. And soon they were all laughing, sharing a joke.

Seeing her sister, Nelle waved and met her at the lockers.

"What were you all laughing at?"

Nelle chuckled.

"Gym class today. We were playing dodgeball and I got hit so hard in the stomach, I landed on my behind. The ball bounced off me and tagged Mrs. P out!" She giggled. "You should've seen her face. You know what a good sport she is!"

There was no ride to meet them when the bus let them off at their stop. George shrugged, hefted his book bag.

"Maybe Daddy will meet us along the way," he suggested. "At least it's not raining."

Pheen sighed, and Nelle nudged her as they set off after him.

"You're awfully quiet. How was your day?"

Pheen sighed again.

"Mae ate lunch with me today." She met her sister's gaze. "Them older girls—Lucille and Lizzie and their friends—were sitting behind me. They were whispering mean stuff, trying to make me mad, I guess."

"About me?"

Pheen nodded.

Her sister sniffed.

"Pay no attention to them. Bunch of hateful gossips, all of them." She bumped her shoulder against Pheen's. "I mean it. I don't let their spitefulness bother me and you shouldn't either. We're the best-looking girls in high school and two of the smartest." She laughed. "And you are definitely smarter than me!"

They had walked two miles home when George whooped.

"Told ya! Here comes Daddy!"

Nelle put her arm around her sister's waist as they waited for the truck to reach them.

"Me and you are going to have better lives than that snotty Lucille, you wait and see. I'm gonna get married to a good man who's going places in this old world, we'll have two kids, and a fine home. You'll probably end up going off to college to be a teacher yourself, Miss Josephine Joy." She let go of Pheen as the truck pulled up. "And Lucille'll be lucky if anybody looks twice at her. She'll end up an old maid living at home and taking care of her parents the rest of their days."

They climbed in the truck cab, Pheen in first. Nelle leaned forward.

"Daddy, you better keep an eye on Pheen here. Some boy's likely to run off and marry her before you know it."

John Keller looked at his second daughter.

"Them boys goggling you at school, Josephine Joy?"

Nelle nodded. "She's the prettiest ninth grader in the whole school. Matthew Childers' eyes bugged out when he got on the bus this morning and saw her."

Pheen blushed.

"He didn't pay me no mind, Daddy. Don't listen to her!"

CHAPTER FIVE

More often than not as the weather grew colder, the old pick-up truck was waiting for them at the bus stop on Route 32. Nan smiled the first time she picked up her three oldest.

"Momma!" George whistled. "I only seen you drive the truck in the field for Daddy!"

"Well, climb on up, George. You're letting the cold air in. We need to get back. Your grandma almost has supper ready."

Nelle pushed Pheen into the truck ahead of her, squeezing in after her along the bench seat.

"We near froze to death on that old bus!" She shivered. "Poor Pheen's teeth were chattering something awful."

"The truck heater's working just fine." Her mother reached across George to pat Pheen's knee. "You all will be toasty before we get home."

"But where's Daddy?"

"Working in the sawmill. Days are getting shorter as winter's coming on." She maneuvered the truck through a muddy stretch of the dirt road. "He needs to get as much work done as he can while there's daylight."

"When I get outta high school," George spoke up, "I'm going to trade school or maybe even to college."

"What would you do in college?" Nelle jeered and rolled her eyes.

"Study engineering, maybe," George retorted. "Mr. Wilson in shop class says I got a real head for figuring out mechanical things." He looked at his mother. "I don't want to work from sun up to sun down farming and timbering."

Their mother kept her eyes on the road ahead and didn't say anything. Pheen bit her lip. She knew her mother was torn. It was true, their father often worked from dawn until after nightfall. Something always needed doing on the farm, and the timber brought in much of the money that kept the farm going. An extra pair of hands would be a big help, but her older brother was happiest when tinkering with something mechanical. Even now, he kept the farm tractor running and the old truck going, too. Lewis, now, was a different story. Pheen smiled at the thought of her younger brother. Somehow, she couldn't see Lewis ever leaving the farming life behind. He was always begging their parents to let him skip school to help out on the farm.

George poked Nelle. "You're so smart, why don't you go to college? Or open a fancy dress shop, the way you're always sewing something." He chuckled. "You think boys don't pay attention? I hear them town girls talking, Nelle. They's all crazy about your clothes."

Nelle tossed her head.

"I'm not gonna have to work when I get out of school, George. I'm planning to marry someone who'll be able to take good care of me and our two kids."

"You got everything all figured out, huh?" George shot back. "You got the lucky guy all picked out, too?"

"As a matter of fact, I just might!"

Pheen kept her thoughts to herself. If Nelle had somebody specific in mind, she sure hadn't confided his name to her sister. And Pheen couldn't think of anyone at school who seemed to have caught Nelle's attention. The taunts of Lucille, Helen, and Lizzie and their friends came back to her—accusing Nelle of chasing after older boys. A senior? Pheen's eyes narrowed. Or maybe a boy no longer in school?

The news just before Christmas worried Pheen. Canadian soldiers had arrived in Britain, and she remembered how President Roosevelt had signed an order increasing the size of America's armed forces back in the fall. It sure seemed like war was coming closer one way or the other. She kept a close eye on George, but he seemed focused on his schoolwork. She thought he wanted their daddy to see how smart he was, that maybe he'd approve of George going on to more schooling after high school. She ate her breakfast and helped clear the table. Her mother gave her a hug.

"What's the matter, honey? You not feeling well?"

Pheen managed a half-smile.

"Just worrying about my history test, that's all, Momma."

She couldn't tell her mother how tired she was. How the cold and the long walk to school—those mornings when they didn't have a ride—sapped her energy. She loved her classes, loved going to high school, loved the praise from her teachers. But she was dreading the next few days—her time of the month was due. Regular as clockwork, heavy, and making her schooldays a nightmare to endure. She thought of her sister with envy. Nelle breezed through those days of the month, while Pheen curled up from cramps, lost sleep because she was always running for the bathroom throughout the night, and couldn't concentrate half the time.

"I've seen how much time you've spent studying. I'm sure you'll do just fine." Her mother handed Pheen her lunch money. "I've given you a little extra, honey.

You treat yourself at lunch. I hear they sometimes have extra hermit cookies!"

Sitting on her bed after supper, arms locked around her knees, Pheen stifled a moan as the ache in her lower back intensified. Nelle paused in the act of adding a pair of socks to the pile of clothing on the bed.

"Do you want me to make you a hot water bottle?"

Pheen shook her head, then moaned again.

"No, it'll pass."

"For heaven's sake, Josephine Joy!" Nelle rolled her eyes and dropped the socks onto the pile. "You sound just like Momma. Lie down and I'll be back in a minute."

Her sister returned as promised with a hot water bottle, two aspirin, and a glass of water.

"Here, take these." While Pheen swallowed the aspirin, her sister plumped up the pillows on the bed and leaned Pheen against them, positioning the hot water bottle across her younger sister's lower back.

"Now isn't that better?"

Pheen nodded.

"No use hurting more than you need to when it's your time of the month." Nelle opened the wardrobe they shared with Virgie and pursed her mouth as she reviewed her clothes. She pulled her best dress from its hanger.

"You can't tell it ever had a ripped seam," Pheen marveled and raised her eyebrows at her sister. "You aren't wearing that dress to school tomorrow?"

Spreading the dress front side down on the bed, Nelle snorted.

"Of course not, silly." She carefully folded the sides of the full skirt in, then the sleeves. Next, the skirt was folded in half, and finally the bodice was folded over the skirt. "I'm going to spend the night with Jenny Pack after school tomorrow. Her daddy is going to drive us back to school for the Christmas dance at eight o'clock."

She gave Pheen a quick look.

"And before you ask, yes, Daddy knows I'm going to the dance. Cousin Alfa and her husband Fred are going to be two of the chaperones. And, Frank and Harry will be there, too. Daddy won't have to worry none about me."

Nelle abandoned her packing and sat down on the bed next to her sister. Smoothing Pheen's hair back from her forehead, she dropped a quick kiss on top of her head.

"I'm sorry you're feeling so poorly. I'll collect your homework assignments and bring them to you, okay?" She bopped Pheen gently on the nose. "If you could go to that old dance wearing that white blouse and black satin skirt I made last year, you'd outshine everybody there, including me!"

"No," Pheen disagreed. "You'll look like a million bucks in your dress, Nelle. Like a movie star!" Frank and Harry, she thought, were going to have their work cut out for them at the dance. George was going, too. He'd spend the night afterwards with Frank and Harry. But he wouldn't be watching Nelle at the dance. He'd be too busy out on the dance floor with half a dozen girls eager to be his partner. Her sister resumed her packing and Pheen turned on her side. She was the only one who wouldn't be going to the Christmas dance. At least her menses had given her an excuse. Unlike her older sister and brother, the thought of going to a dance made her feel self-conscious. It was hard enough to be the youngest kid in her class!

George and Nelle were in high spirits when Frank dropped them at home on Saturday, making Grandma Lavinia chuckle as they jitterbugged around the dining room.

"Looks like you all had a fine time at the Christmas dance last night!"

Grabbing his grandmother by the hand, George swung her about as Pheen and Nelle clapped and sang, "Sing, sing, sing, sing, everybody start to sing!"

"You'll make a jitterbugger yet, Grandma!" George laughed as he twirled her about.

"Me next, George!" Virgie tugged at his arm. "Watch me! I can dance, too!"

George spun Virgie about as Grandma Lavinia sat down and fanned herself with her apron.

"Lordy!"

Nelle touched Pheen on the arm.

"C'mon upstairs while I unpack and change clothes." As they headed for the living room and the stairs, she tossed over her shoulder. "Wait till you hear what that old Lucille Prater wore to the dance!"

"Pink? With ruffles??" Nelle was lying across her bed in jeans and a sweater, the latest copy of *Photoplay* opened to a photo of Clark Gable. "We're talking Pepto-Bismol pink, Pheen. It was that dress in the window we saw when we were in Louisa before Thanksgiving, remember?" She sat up and crossed her legs. "And she added a fat ole ribbon around the waist, tied in a bow so big her partners couldn't get close to her. If they'd wanted to," she added and turned the page of her magazine. "Ohh, look at this!" She held up the magazine to show Pheen a photo of Victor McLaglen and sighed. "He's so handsome!"

"Momma's partial to Gary Cooper," Pheen commented. "So who did you dance with? Did Mae come? Or was it just Lizzie?"

"Oh, Mae had a cold, Lizzie said. She and Hobart came."

"Did you dance with Hobart?"

Nelle turned another page. "Hobart's not much of a jitterbugger."

Supper was long over when Pheen cut two slices of their grandmother's leftover apple pie and set one before George at the small kitchen table. She took her own plate and sat across from him.

"You shoulda seen it, the gym was all decorated. There was punch and cake, too! It was a swell party." He took a bite of his pie.

"Nelle said Lizzie and Hobart came."

George looked up from his pie. "She should know, she spent about half the night dancing with him."

"She told me he wasn't much of a jitterbugger."

"They were dancing all the slow dances together." He frowned. "All the guys wanted to dance with her. Frank and Harry each took a turn—those two cats can swing!" He grinned at his sister. "But that Hobart!" The grin disappeared. "Thinks he's too good or something. He'll be making tracks if Daddy ever catches him making eyes at Nelle."

Pheen's fork stopped midway to her mouth. George shook his head.

"I don't know what Nelle was thinking. She and Howie Jones could win a contest jitterbugging! I mean it, they was that good! Hobart didn't like it one bit, I could tell." He finished his pie and laughed. "He'd better try harder at jitterbugging, if he aims to keep up with Nelle!"

CHAPTER SIX
1940

"Hattie McDaniel deserved that Oscar," Grandma Lavinia pronounced with a stern eye for George. The breakfast table conversation was all about *Gone With the Wind* and how it had won so many Oscars in late February.

"I didn't say anything," George protested and helped himself to more scrambled eggs and another biscuit.

"C'mon, George, admit it, you would've voted for Olivia de Havilland to win!" Nelle insisted. "I've seen you mooning over her picture!"

"I just think it's a shame Claudette Colbert didn't even get nominated," he muttered, buttering his biscuit. "That *Drums Along the Mohawk* movie was cool—all those battles and history and…" he swallowed a bite, "…and Indians, too!"

Pheen worked her way steadily through a small plateful of bacon and eggs and kept her thoughts to herself. The news on the radio last night had been grim: Mussolini had joined up with Hitler. There seemed to be a steady beat of war moving through Europe. Where would it end? When? At least if George had his mind on the movies, he wasn't planning to run off to Canada anytime soon. As if to confirm her thoughts, he picked up his plate and stood.

"That new Bob Hope and Bing Crosby movie's supposed to be real good."

"*The Road to Singapore*?" Nelle pushed back her chair.

"Yeah, can't wait till it comes to the theater in Louisa."

Nelle called over her shoulder as she and George took their breakfast dishes into the kitchen, "Quit dawdling, Pheen. Hobart's giving us a ride to school today—all the way into Louisa. We won't have to ride the bus this morning."

Pheen stood up slowly. Having a ride to school was a relief, but she didn't relish Hobart's driving. An extra hard bump reminded her why as Hobart drove along the curves and hills of the road that followed Brushy Creek. He liked to show-off, it seemed to her. Taking the curves a little fast, bouncing the car on the rutted road.

Lizzie, sitting up front with Hobart and Mae, set her mouth in a hard line.

"Slow down, Hobart! You are doing this on purpose!"

He laughed and hit the next rut even faster. Each time he sped up, he looked in the rearview mirror to see how Nelle reacted. When Nelle laughed, Lizzie's mouth set even harder. If looks could kill, Pheen figured Hobart would've been a goner. For the backseat passengers, it was like riding a rollercoaster, and Pheen was left feeling queasy by the time Hobart dropped them off at the high school.

Mae joined Pheen at lunch, like she'd done every day since her schedule had changed. She opened her lunch bag and shook her head.

"Mama's sent a bread and butter sandwich with an apple and a big slice of that chocolate cake she made on Sunday." Mae stood up. "I'm going to get some of that stew and a bottle of milk, Pheen. I'm hungry, but I can't eat all that cake." She looked sadly at the cake. "Lizzie says it'll give me spots and I'll get fat."

"You won't get fat eating a piece of cake!" Pheen declared. "Go on, I've already got some stew. It's good today!"

Mae came back with her food and sat down with another sigh.

"Lizzie's always criticizing me about something." She looked horrified at what she'd just said. "I mean, she's my sister. She's just looking out for me." She took a bite of her stew. "Like, this outfit I'm wearing today. Lizzie said it's perfect for me, but I don't know." Her shoulders dropped and she lowered her voice. "Lucille and Helen're always making fun of how I look."

Today Lizzie sat with Lucille and Helen and their group of girlfriends at a table across the cafeteria, their heads together. They kept glancing at the group of senior boys at the next table and whispering and giggling among themselves.

Pheen surveyed her friend. Mae was wearing a mustard yellow plaid dress with a brown cardigan. Her hair had been bobbypinned to create waves, but her curls were frizzy instead of lying in soft waves. Pheen finished off her sandwich.

"Listen, Mae," she began cautiously, not sure how the other girl would react. "Sometimes we think other people will look good if they dress just like us." She pointed to Mae's dress. "I bet Lizzie picked it out," she paused as Mae nodded. "And I bet that color would look fine on her. But you know what, that forest green plaid skirt you wore last week? You should wear more colors like that. And that dark red dress of yours with the navy blue trim, Nelle said it really suits you."

Mae beamed.

"And Nelle helps me with my hair," she shrugged, "or it wouldn't ever have a curl. You have beautiful thick hair, but I bet it's hard to get it really curly."

"You said it!" Mae ran a hand through her hair. "I can't ever get it to look like the pictures in the magazines."

"If I was you," Pheen studied her friend's face for a moment, then offered, "I'd make a side part, pin the ends into fat curls after you wash your hair. When they're dry, comb the curls under and use a barrette to hold this side off your face." She demonstrated on her own hair.

"And I don't think you could ever get fat, even if you ate the whole cake!"

"Here," Mae used her fork to cut her slice of cake in half. "We'll share!" She took a bite. "Mmm, so good!" She took another bite. "Nelle really said that about my red dress?"

Pheen nodded.

"She's the best-dressed girl in the whole school!" Mae declared.

Now it was Pheen's turn to beam.

All the kids on the bus were buzzing about the World's Fair reopening in New York and how they wished they could go see it, but Pheen's forehead was creased in a frown. The Germans had bombed England and invaded France. She couldn't stop thinking about what that might mean. Her daddy remained convinced that the war wouldn't touch them, but she wondered who he was trying to convince—himself or the rest of his family? Grandma Lavinia listened to the news every night, shook her head, and turned to her bible.

"What was it like, Grandma?" Pheen asked. The two of them were sharing the swing out on the front porch after supper. The late May night was warm, the air scented by the roses climbing a trellis at the edge of the porch behind them. "During World War I?"

Her grandma stilled for a long moment, then gently began rocking the swing once more.

"It was hard times," the old woman gathered her thoughts, her voice quiet. "Young men went off to fight. Some of them are still there—buried far from home and their kin."

"I'm sorry, Grandma," Pheen rested her head against her grandmother's shoulder. "I didn't mean to make you sad."

"I know why you're asking, and I know what you're not asking." Lavinia put an arm around Pheen and pulled her close. "I do think we'll be at war again. There's too much evil in this world for us to stay clear of it for long." Laying her cheek against her granddaughter's head, she sighed again. "I wish it could be different, but I won't lie to you. War's coming, I feel it in my bones."

Nelle stood in front of the bureau's mirror, applying lipstick to her lower lip with care. Pheen brushed Virgie's hair and gave her younger sister a pat on the bottom.

"Now you're all ready for the last day of school, little Miss Virginia Keller! Scoot downstairs and get some breakfast."

"I've already had breakfast," Nelle informed Pheen after blotting her lips on a tissue. She pulled some clean underwear and socks from a drawer. "I'm spending the night with Jenny. Momma said I could," she threw a look over her shoulder at her sister, "so don't wait for me after school."

Pheen's brows shot up. This was the first she'd heard of Nelle's plans. Jenny Pack lived in town, a short walk from the high school. And a short walk from the dance hall in Louisa, too. Pheen had heard the older girls chattering in the cafeteria about a dance to be held on the last day of school.

"You and Jenny going to that dance tonight?"

"I'm sure I don't know what you're talking about, Josephine Joy." Nelle picked up her bag. "C'mon, hurry. Hobart doesn't like to be kept waiting."

"I'm talking about the dance everybody at school was jabbering about yesterday!" Pheen hissed as she followed Nelle downstairs. Her sister ignored her as a horn sounded in the lane.

"Bye, Momma!" Nelle blew a kiss at their mother. "See you tomorrow!"

Hobart hit another quick tap-tap-tap on his horn and revved the engine. George came out the door on Pheen's heels.

"He sure don't like to wait, does he?"

Mae got out and climbed into the backseat, throwing a look of confusion at her brother as she did. George held the door for Pheen, who slid in after Mae, then jumped in after his sister. Nelle seated herself in the front seat.

"Where's Lizzie?" Nelle asked as Hobart backed out onto the lane and headed down the road.

It was Mae who answered. "She's got a bad stomachache," she said and her face reddened as she glanced at George. Pheen understood what Mae didn't want to say. Today was Awards' Day, and Lizzie wasn't up for a single award. Mae was getting an award for winning the school spelling bee and one for perfect attendance, too.

"Don't be nervous today, Mae," she reassured her friend. "You look great!" Mae had taken to wearing her hair as Pheen had suggested. She'd even cut it a few inches shorter in length, so her curls lay on her shoulders. She was wearing a short-sleeved white blouse with a simple navy cotton skirt. "Is that a new skirt?"

Mae smiled. "Daddy got it for me on account of me winning the spelling bee." Her eyes were shining.

"You deserve it, Mae!" George nodded. "It don't take no work just to come to school every day, but to win the Ninth Grade Spelling Bee, you have to study!"

"You saying my little sister isn't smart, George Keller?" Hobart challenged as he swerved the car to miss a rabbit bounding across the road.

George's face turned beet red.

"No, I never meant any such thing, Mae!" He cleared his throat. "I just meant you had to put in time to learn all them new words!"

Nelle laughed.

"Calm down, George! He's just teasing. Aren't you, Hobart?"

Hobart's laugh sounded forced.

"Sure, sure! Just pulling your leg, Keller!"

CHAPTER SEVEN

"I'll thank you to mind your own business, George Keller!" Nelle's voice was sharp. "Last time I looked, you are not my daddy!"

Pheen stood frozen in the upstairs hallway. She'd just woken up and gotten dressed. Now that it was warm enough, the two summer bedrooms off the second-story back porch were open—Nelle having claimed one and George the other. Being the oldest, they had dibs on the rooms as long as no family was visiting from out-of-state.

"Half the guys in high school are making eyes at you," George's voice was low, but determined. "I'm telling you, Nelle, that Hobart's got a temper on him! I don't want you getting hurt!"

"And I'll say it again," came his sister's hot reply. "Mind your own business. Hobart isn't afraid to stand up for himself, is all." She turned, saw Pheen standing in the hallway, and brushed past her, her cat in her arms. "Close your mouth, Pheen, before you swallow a fly! And you can mind your own business, too!" She bounded down the stairs before Pheen could do more than sputter and close her mouth.

George came down the hallway slowly and paused by his younger sister.

"I don't get it," he said. "Nelle can pretty much go with any guy from school. Howie Jones is nuts about her and he's a swell guy!"

Pheen shrugged and followed her brother downstairs. She shared his misgivings about Hobart, but Nelle sure wasn't going to listen to her if she brushed off George's concern.

"She'll get tired of him, you wait and see," she told George. "I don't care for him either, nor Lizzie, if you want to know what I think."

"Mae's okay," George muttered. Pheen smiled behind his back.

"She's much nicer than her sister," she agreed, "and cute as a button, too!"

George mumbled something she didn't catch as they passed through the living room to the dining room. Nelle's cat twined about Pheen's legs and followed her into the kitchen. Nelle was nowhere to be seen.

"Nelle went out to gather the eggs," her mother remarked as Pheen opened the screen door and let the cat out. "What's got her flouncing around so early this morning?"

Pheen shrugged. "She and George were arguing when I got up. He probably asked her to iron his shirt again," she offered, hoping to divert her mother's attention.

"One of these days, that boy'd better learn to iron his own shirts!" Grandma Lavinia spoke up as she took a pan of biscuits from the oven.

"That'll be the day!" Pheen scoffed and laughed. "George is too particular about his clothes!"

Her mother laughed. "He'd better marry someone, then, that knows how to iron."

"Or wants to iron!"

George chose that moment to walk into the kitchen, holding his shirt.

"Momma, look here! A button's hanging by a thread on this shirt I was gonna wear today."

Pheen, his grandmother, and his mother burst into laughter.

"What?" he asked, bewildered. "What are you all laughing at?"

"Put the shirt in my mending basket, George. I'll sew it on for you later," his mother said.

George went out of the kitchen, shaking his head.

Grandma Lavinia chuckled. "Here Pheen, put these biscuits on the table. Go tell Virgie and Lewis that breakfast is ready."

Carrying a pail, Pheen followed Nelle into the woods along the edge of the bottom where their daddy's tobacco allotment grew. Black raspberries were hanging on the vines now, and she and Nelle were planning to fill their pails. Some of the berries would be eaten with fresh churned vanilla ice cream, or Grandma Lavinia might bake a pound cake if the kitchen wasn't too hot this evening.

"Here's a good patch!" Nelle stopped and pointed at the thicket ahead of them. Both were wearing blue jeans and long-sleeved poplin shirts against the briars. For a few minutes, the only sound heard was that of berries plunking into their pails. It was hot, the thicket holding in the heat of the day. A mosquito whined near Pheen's ear and she swatted at it.

"Did you and Jenny have fun at that dance the last day of school?" she ventured, casting a quick look at her sister. Nelle hadn't said a word about the dance, although Pheen was sure she'd gone.

Nelle kept her eyes on the berries in front of her, moving a long arching cane out of her face before answering.

"We did," she answered and now she glanced at Pheen. "What you really want to know is if Hobart was there. Yes, he was. And furthermore, I saw him at the store in Blaine yesterday and he asked me to go to the show with him this Saturday. I said I would." As Pheen's eyes widened, her sister sighed. "Don't worry, Frank and Harry are taking me to town and going to the movie with their girlfriends. It's not like I'm going on a date alone!"

She picked some more berries before adding, "And you can bet if that old Lizzie finds out Hobart's going to the show, she'll make a fuss about coming, too!"

Pheen didn't say anything, kept picking berries with her head bent. Nelle spoke up after a moment.

"Listen, if Lizzie invites herself along, I'll make sure Mae comes, too." She smiled as Pheen looked up. "And then you can come. Heck, George can come if he wants! That'll fix Lizzie." Nelle chuckled.

Later, pails brimming, the girls headed home. As they crossed the bottom, Nelle broke their silence.

"I know you don't much like Hobart, Pheen." Nelle went on as Pheen grimaced and didn't say anything. "But he's fun when you get to know him. And he goes to church every Sunday and he's got a job already." She turned to her sister, her voice light. "That's how we're going to the movies—Hobart's treat!"

"George says," Pheen started and Nelle held up a hand.

"Oh hush! George is our brother!" She laughed. "He's supposed to fuss over us, Pheen! Wouldn't matter what boy you liked! You wait and see," she predicted, "wait until you like some boy." Nelle stopped dead in her tracks. "Come to think of it," she examined Pheen with narrowed eyes, "I've seen Matthew talking to you a few times at school!"

Flushing, Pheen stammered. "He was in my math class! That's all, honest to goodness!"

"Uh huh!" Nelle picked up her pace. "C'mon, let's get these berries home. I'm hot and Momma was going to make a pitcher of lemonade."

George, it turned out, was under the old pick-up truck on Saturday afternoon.

"Daddy says," he told Pheen, sliding half-way out from under the truck to wipe the sweat and oil from his face, "if I can get this old baby running, he'll give me enough money from the tobacco sales to keep it going for a while." His eyes shining, he added. "Just think, Pheen! No more long walks to the bus stop. No trudging home in the rain and cold next year!" He stuffed his handkerchief into his overall pocket. "You said Frank and Harry are taking you all into town for the movie?"

Pheen nodded.

"Well, then," he shot her a look, "that'll be okay then." He slid back under the pick-up. "Let me know if the movie's worth seeing." He chortled. "'Cause I'm going to have this here truck running in no time. Then I can drive us to the show!"

Mae had come along with Hobart when he met up with Nelle and Pheen in front of the movie theater. Lizzie, it turned out, was spending the weekend with her cousins. Watching him, Pheen could tell he was pleased to have Lizzie out of his way for once. Standing in line at the concession booth with Mae, Pheen saw Nelle at the end of the line, waving. Frank and Harry had arrived with their steady girls—Julia Smith and Howie Jone's older sister, Susie. They huddled with Nelle and Hobart.

"I'm getting a box of *Goobers*," Mae decided. "I really like popcorn at the movies, but I get so thirsty!"

Pheen nodded, "Same for me—about the popcorn, I mean. I'll have a *Baby Ruth*," she told the attendant and paid for her candy.

"You go on ahead," Nelle called to her sister. "We'll find you after the show."

With a quick look at Nelle, Pheen followed Mae into the theater. Nelle might have managed to ditch her little sister, Pheen noticed, but Frank and Harry would keep an eye on her. Then again, after seeing the way Julia and Susie were watching her cousins, she wasn't sure either one of the guys would have an eye to spare for Nelle.

Just before the lights went down, Nelle and Hobart made their way up the aisle to the back of the theater. Frank and Julia were ahead of them and Harry and Susie behind them. Pheen grinned to herself. Hobart better mind his ps and qs. A *Tom & Jerry* cartoon began, Mae started giggling, and Pheen, confident that Frank and Harry were on the job, settled in to enjoy the show. The Three Stooges in *You Nazty Spy*! was playing, having been released way back in January and was just now being shown locally. George, she decided, would love it.

"That was a fun movie!" Nelle declared. "I laughed so hard my sides ached." They were standing outside the theater in the afternoon sun. "Susie, tell Howie hello for me. That brother of yours sure can jitterbug!"

"That's all he thinks about, that and—" Susie caught herself after a quick look at Nelle and laughed.

Hobart's face was blotchy as he took Mae by the arm.

"Gotta get my sister home. Good seeing you guys," he nodded at Frank and Harry. "C'mon, Mae. I'm parked down there near the hotel." He turned to Nelle. "See you, Nelle."

Julia Smith's eyes widened as she looked from Nelle to Hobart.

"We're going to grab a bite at the Dixie Diner," she told Hobart. "Why don't you and Mae come along?"

Mae opened her mouth, then closed it as Hobart forced a smile.

"Not today. Like I said, I gotta get Mae home."

Nelle went straight to her room as soon as they got home. George waylaid Pheen.

"I got the truck purring like a kitten," he reported with a grin. "So how was that movie?"

"As funny as you'd expect," she told him. "You'll like it!"

She made her way up to the room she shared with Virgie and sat for a moment, indecisive. Nelle had barely said a word on the ride home. Making up her mind, Pheen headed down the hallway to Nelle's bedroom. The door was closed and even as she raised her hand to knock, she stopped. From within she could hear muffled sobs, as if Nelle's face were buried in her pillow. Troubled, Pheen backed away from the door.

CHAPTER EIGHT

Mrs. Sarah Jenkins stood on the front porch, fiddling with the clasp on her heavy black pocketbook, a bag clutched under one arm.

"You did a fine job cutting this dress down for Mary," she told Nelle. Her eyes followed her daughter, who was playing hopscotch with Virgie on the walk which led to a gate in the fence that enclosed the front yard. "Her cousin Matilda is a mite bigger than my girl." Her hands told the story of why Sarah could not sew for her daughter herself. The knuckles of both hands were red and swollen with the rheumatism. Pheen, sitting in the wicker rocker, flinched at the sight of those hands and rubbed her knuckles in sympathy.

Nelle dropped onto the seat of the rocker next to her sister as Mrs. Jenkins collected Mary and went out the gate to the car idling in the lane. Mr. Jenkins tooted the horn once and Mary waved to Virgie as they drove away.

"'A mite bigger,' my foot!" Nelle rolled her eyes and laughed. "Tildy Jenkins might be the same age as her cousin, but she's at least twice the size of Mary!" She stuffed the money Mrs. Jenkins had paid her into the pocket of her jeans. "That dress fits Mary to a T—nobody will ever guess she's wearing Tildy's hand-me-downs! I made sure of that." She smiled. "I doubt Miz Jenkins will notice, but I made some changes to that dress. It don't look like the original at all."

"I reckon George is right," Pheen returned her sister's smile. "Why, you could probably open your own business right now!" Pursing her lips, she watched the cloud of dust stirred along the road as the Jenkins drove away. "You could do alterations, there's other women like poor Miz Jenkins. Did you see her hands?" Pheen shuddered and sat up straighter. "You know there's other women don't do none of their own sewing."

Nelle shook her head before Pheen had finished speaking.

"I'm not slaving away in a shop altering clothes for the likes of big-headed women like Delia Cordle or Alice Prater," she said firmly. "Putting on airs at church, no less! Acting like they're better than Momma!"

Virgie came up the steps to the porch and squeezed into the chair with Nelle.

"That sure was a pretty dress you made for Mary!" She leaned against her sister. "You should make me a nicer one, Nelle. Please! Pretty please?" She sat up as Nelle didn't say anything. "You make Pheen clothes!"

Pheen stood up.

"You're a big baby, Virgie! Nelle got paid to fix that dress for Mary. Who's gonna pay her to make you a dress?"

"I hate you, Pheen! You are so mean!" Virgie's lower lip stuck out. "Nelle can use that money to buy me a new dress! She won't even have to sew it!"

Nelle sighed, moved her little sister, and got up. "I got plans for that money, Virgie. You know Daddy will buy you a new dress for school if he can."

Virgie's wails followed her older sisters as they went into the house.

"Momma! Momma! Nelle and Pheen're being mean to me!"

Pheen gave Nelle a curious look. "What plans? What are you up to, Nelle?"

Nelle stopped at the newel post and eyed Pheen. "Nothing you need to know, Josephine Joy!" Then she laughed, turned to run lightly up the staircase, and threw over her shoulder. "I just want some money saved, that's all. I'll be graduating school in a little over a years' time, you know. Don't worry about me!"

At the bottom of the stairs, Pheen watched Nelle disappear from sight as she made her way up the stairs and turned down the upstairs hallway towards the summer bedrooms. Shrugging, she headed for the kitchen and the pitcher of lemonade sure to be found in the refrigerator.

George managed to keep the old farm truck running, for which Pheen was profoundly grateful. Colder weather came and with it rainy days, but the weather was only a problem if the lane that took them to Route 32 was washed out when Brushy Creek overflowed its banks. Even rutted as the lane could get, George managed to steer the old truck through the deepest, muddiest ruts.

"Road's better today," George grunted. It was early November and they'd had a colder few days, but dry. "We'll make good time to Louisa this morning."

A horn honked as a car came down the road behind them, going fast. George hugged the hillside, but there was no place to pull over. He looked back with annoyance.

"It's Arnett! I swear, what's he in such an all-fired hurry for?"

The horn sounded again, longer this time. Pheen glanced back, any closer and Hobart's car would be pushing them down the road. Nelle, sitting in the middle, looked straight ahead. George managed to get the truck farther to the right as Hobart pulled around them and gunned his car. The car bounced as he swerved in front of them and Pheen could see Mae's face, her hand over her mouth, and caught a glimpse of Lizzie's angry face as the car roared away from them.

"That fool's gonna get somebody killed one of these days!" George muttered.

"Serve him right if it's him," Nelle spoke for the first time.

Wide-eyed, Pheen exchanged a look with George behind Nelle's back. George winked. Pheen looked with interest at her sister, Nelle hadn't gone to the movies with Hobart since the day Mae and Pheen had tagged along. Maybe, the thought came with a small rush of relief, maybe Nelle was done with him forever.

"Let's hope no one else is in the car with him then," Pheen said, and sat back on the bench seat.

With the *Big Sandy* newspaper spread out on the bed before her, Pheen looked up as Nelle came in and sat on the bed, her hair in pincurls with a scarf tied around her head.

"What're you reading that old rag for?"

"It says here the Germans are still bombing Britain. It's almost Thanksgiving, Nelle. When's it going to stop?" She rolled over and sat up. "They've been dropping bombs since school started in September."

Nelle shrugged. "You're a worrywart. We're not at war. The Germans wouldn't dare drop any bombs on us." She yawned and changed the subject. "Howie and I are gonna win that dance contest at school on Friday, you wait and see." She hopped off the bed and went to the wardrobe. "Help me think of something to wear!"

Nelle started pulling out dresses, blouses, and skirts, and laying them out on the bed.

"You know what would look good on you?" Pheen ventured. "That blue dress Daddy got Momma last Christmas. The two of you are about the same size."

Nelle considered as Pheen added. "Go on, ask her if you can try it on."

"It does have a great skirt," Nelle admitted. "Easy to dance in. You're a genius, Pheen!"

Pheen sat on the sidelines, excited as the rest of the school crowd when Howie and Nelle took the dance floor. Nelle had indeed worn her mother's blue dress, her golden curls held back with a matching ribbon. Her cheeks were flushed, her eyes bright, and she and Howie never missed a beat. Of course they won, Pheen cheered as the winners were announced. Refreshments had been set up in the cafeteria adjacent to the gymnasium where the competition was held. Nelle joined her sister, while Howie made a beeline for the punch bowl and Sherrilee Casteel.

"I thought Howie liked you!" Pheen said before she thought, but Nelle laughed and shrugged. "That was last year. We're just dance partners." She gestured at the two teenagers across the room, their heads close together over cups of punch. "He and Sherrilee are going steady. They make a cute couple, don't you think?"

"George says Jerry Thompson thinks you're cute, Nelle. Maybe he'll ask you to the Christmas dance."

"Oh, he's okay," Nelle answered. "But Jenny and I are going by ourselves." She eyed her sister. "What about you? I hear Matthew Childers and Jimmy Thompson nearly had a fistfight over which one of them was gonna ask you to the dance!"

Pheen choked on her cookie. "Neither—neither one of them has asked me. You made that up, Elanor Rose!"

Nelle chuckled. "You wait and see, Pheen, wait and see!"

The first package showed up on the front porch about a week before Christmas—a small box about six inches square, wrapped in newspaper with Nelle's name written on it. Lewis found it when he opened the door to call Ruby.

"Look here, Nelle! This has your name written on it," he hollered.

Nelle came in from the dining room and snatched the package from her brother.

"Hey!" Lewis protested. "I wasn't going to open it!"

"Who's it from, huh?" he asked, forgetting Ruby and dogging Nelle's steps back to the dining table. "Look everybody! Nelle's got a present from somebody secret!"

"I want to see!" Virgie jumped up from her chair. "Let me open it, Nelle!"

Nelle tucked the package into her pocket, sat down, and picked up her fork.

"Not everything's for you, Virgie. Sit down."

Her mother walked in with a basket of hot biscuits and put them on the breakfast table. She gave Nelle an amused look as Virgie opened her mouth to protest.

"Your sister's right, Virginia," her mother ordered. "Sit down, please." Though she phrased the order pleasantly, Virgie knew when she was defeated and sat. Pheen saw her lower lip jutting out and figured Virgie would try and wheedle the package away from Nelle later.

"It's probably somebody's idea of a joke," Nelle declared. "And I'm not going to open it in front of a bunch of nosey-parkers." She broke a biscuit onto her plate and spooned sausage gravy over the top of the crumbled biscuit.

"That's right," Grandma Lavinia admonished the rest of the table's occupants. "You all need to mind your own business, finish your breakfast, and get ready for school." She laid a hand on Lewis' arm. "And that includes you, young man. Ruby won't starve to death if you take five minutes to eat your own breakfast first."

He slid back into his chair.

"Yes, ma'am!" He grinned and accepted a helping of scrambled eggs from the bowl George passed to him.

Pheen, sitting across the table from her sister, watched as Nelle calmly finished her biscuit and gravy, then took a second biscuit and buttered it before adding a liberal amount of strawberry jam. She glanced up, saw Pheen watching her, and winked. Pheen relaxed. Whoever it was from, Nelle would likely tell her anyway, joke or no joke.

But Nelle didn't share the giver's identity—not then, nor the next day or throughout the rest of the week leading up to Christmas day, when small packages continued to appear on the front porch. No matter how quick George and Lewis tried to be, they caught no glimpse of the person leaving them. After the first one, Nelle took each package to her room, locked the door to keep Virgie out, and said not a word when she emerged. And though Virgie snooped, she found no trace of whatever was in each box.

Pheen found Nelle upstairs midafternoon on Christmas Eve, sprawled on her bed with the most recent issue of *Photoplay* open on her lap, her cat asleep beside her. When Pheen walked in, she was staring off into space.

Pheen plopped down on her own bed.

"I just helped Momma with the peanut brittle. The fun part is cracking it into pieces when it's cooled." She held out her hand. "I brought you a piece."

Nelle eyed the proffered candy and grunted. "Thanks." She reached for Pheen's offering and grinned. "I'm still not telling you anything!" She sat back down and took a bite of the candy. "Mmm, this is so good!" Fussing with the pillows behind her back, she leaned back and sighed.

"Listen, Pheen, you gotta promise not to tell a soul." She put out a hand as Pheen's eyes widened. "No, it's nothing bad, for goodness sake! I just don't want no lecturing from George. Or you. Or anybody!"

Pheen nodded.

"It's Hobart. Hobart's been sending me those boxes." She smiled. "And there wasn't nothing in them but a little treat—like a Mars bar, stuff like that." She paused, took a breath. "And a note. The first one was an apology."

"Whatever for?" Pheen asked, startled.

"You remember when we went to the movies last summer?"

Pheen nodded.

"Hobart got fresh with me before the movie ended."

"No!" Pheen's mouth fell open in shock.

"Oh, it wasn't anything horrible, silly, but I'm not that kind of girl. And I told him that and I meant it." She finished her candy. "So I ignored him all summer. I figured if he really liked me, he'd stop being sore and apologize."

Hugging her knees to her chest, Pheen spoke before she thought.

"Stop being sore because he didn't get what he wanted? What a chump!"

Nelle sat up, tossing her magazine aside.

"He's not a chump! You don't understand!" She stood up and gathered her cat into her arms. "I shouldn't have said anything to you!" She stalked out of the bedroom, leaving Pheen to wonder what messages Hobart might have sent in the other boxes.

CHAPTER NINE
1941

Standing in line in the lunchroom, Pheen picked up a tray and eyed the lunch ladies ladling up soup. Tomato soup, it looked like. Her favorite, especially with lots of crackers to crush into her bowl. As the line began to move, someone bumped into her from behind. Annoyed, she looked around to see Matthew Childers blushing deep red.

"Sorry!" he choked out and turned around to swipe at Junior Jones behind him. Junior fended him off, grinning. "Soup looks good," Matthew managed. "Tomato's my favorite."

"Mine, too," Pheen allowed, feeling her cheeks grow red. She could hear Junior sniggering when she turned around as the line moved forward again.

Mae leaned in close as Pheen set her tray down. "Poor Matthew! He looked like he could sink through the floor when Junior pushed him." She rolled her eyes. "I saw that! He did it on purpose! Junior, I mean. So Matthew would bump into you." She bit into her sandwich as Pheen dipped a spoon into her soup.

"He's cute, don't you think?"

"Who?" Pheen pretended not to understand.

"Matthew!" Mae grinned. "I won't tease you." She looked around the lunchroom to where the sophomore boys were seated. "Those boys are always cutting up!"

Pheen finished her soup.

"You should come to the dance next week," Mae spoke into the silence. "We could go together, and maybe George would give us a ride." At the mention of her brother's name, a slight flush washed over Mae's cheeks.

Pheen shook her head.

"Thanks, but I don't think so."

"You should, you really should," Mae insisted. "Nelle's going, isn't she?"

"Nelle and George never miss a dance," Pheen shrugged. "They love to try out all the new steps."

No one had asked her to the Christmas dance, no one had asked her to any dance. Mae, like her sister and brother, went more often than not.

"Say you'll come!" Mae urged. "It'll be fun!"

"I'm not Nelle. I'm the 'smart one,' remember?" She tried to keep her voice light. "Besides, Grandma Lavinia's not feeling well—she's had the bronchitis since the New Year. I've been sitting with her most nights."

Mae touched Pheen's arm.

"I surely understand, Pheen, I do." She pushed away the rest of her sandwich. "My Grandma passed when I was little, but I miss her still." She looked away for a moment. "Grandma was good to me."

Pheen thought she understood what Mae hadn't put into words. Lizzie got most of the attention in that family, and Hobart, too, being the only boy and the oldest.

"Since Hobart and Nelle started going steady, he doesn't want me tagging along to the dances," Mae laughed. "I only get to go if Lizzie makes a fuss about going."

"Nelle and Hobart are really going steady?" Pheen couldn't help herself, her voice rose in surprise.

"I…I think so. I mean, he gave her his class ring."

The bell sounded the end of lunch period. Grabbing her tray, Pheen headed for the window to hand in her dishes. Mae followed.

"I thought you knew, I'm sorry!"

It was warm enough now to sit out on the porch evenings. Pheen caught Nelle alone on the porch that night after supper. Their father and George were listening to the news on the radio, their momma was in the bedroom with Grandma Lavinia. Pheen could hear the old woman coughing and their momma's low voice. Virgie and Lewis were already in bed. Nelle sat curled up in one of the wicker rockers, idly leafing through a magazine even though the dim porch light didn't throw that much light out.

"Are you going steady with Hobart?"

Nelle's head jerked up.

"Who told you that?"

"Never mind. Are you?"

For an answer, Nelle slipped a finger under the collar of her shirt and tugged a chain out A heavy ring hung on the end of it. She smiled.

"As a matter of fact, Miss Nosey-Parker, I am."

"Why're you keeping it a secret?"

"You know why," Nelle hissed, her voice low, "and you better not run telling tales to Momma and Daddy either!" She snapped her magazine closed. "You all hate Hobart, that's why! Well, I'm nearly sixteen now, and nobody's gonna tell me who I can like!"

"That's not fair," Pheen argued. "Nobody hates Hobart!"

"George does!"

"George thinks Hobart's a bully. That's not the same as hating him." Pheen held the swing steady with her toes. "And you know I wouldn't tell on you. I never have, have I?" She was hurt now, and she knew her voice showed it. Nelle got up from her rocker and came to sit by Pheen, putting an arm around her shoulders and pulling her sister close. Resting her chin on the top of Pheen's head, she sighed.

"I'm sorry, Pheen. Sometimes I feel like the whole world is against me."

Pheen buried her head against Nelle's shoulder. "I just don't want to see you get hurt, that's all," she mumbled.

"Nobody's gonna hurt me." She held Pheen tighter. "I know what I'm doing. Hobart's a good man, he'd never do anything to hurt me."

Pheen sat up and wiped her eyes.

"He better not. Or he'd have more than George to worry about!"

"Okay, you little spitfire, calm down!" Nelle laughed. "Let's see if there's any of that icebox cake left before we go up to bed."

Nelle's sixteenth birthday came after school let out for the summer. To celebrate, their daddy took the whole family to the Dixie Diner for supper in Louisa, followed by cake and ice cream at home.

"This here's for you, Nelle," he told his oldest, handing her a small box with a broad smile.

Nelle squealed when she opened it. Virgie crowded close.

"Let me see! Let me see, Nelle!"

Nelle tilted the box up so everyone could see. Inside was an oval cameo brooch, the image worked in ivory set on a black background, surrounded by a narrow braid of gold.

"That belonged to my daddy's mother. She gave it to me before she passed."

"Oh!" Nelle exclaimed softly. "Thank you, Daddy!" She jumped up and came around the table to hug him. He pulled her down on his lap.

"You're my first-born, Elanor Rose, and I know I've said this many a time, but you take after her." He looked around the table at his family. "Grandma Keller was a feisty one, just like our Nelle!" He set her on her feet. "Now open the rest of your presents before Virgie does it for you."

Grandma Lavinia had embroidered a set of dainty handkerchiefs with violets for her granddaughter. George's gift turned out to be a small, rectangular wooden box of walnut, sanded and polished until it shone, with Nelle's initials carved into the top.

"For all your treasures," he told her as she opened it. "I made it in shop class this year."

Virgie produced a necklace of plastic beads that she'd gotten at the Lawrence County fair last year.

"I love it!" Nelle exclaimed and carefully pulled the strand of beads over her head.

"Nelle likes my present best!" Virgie crowed. "It's red, Nelle. Your favorite color!"

Lewis held out a rolled up sheet of paper.

"It's not much, I hope you like it."

With care, Nelle unrolled it on the table and gasped.

"Why, Lewis!" She reached an arm around her younger brother and pulled him close.

"Look everybody!" She held the paper up.

Lewis had drawn a portrait of Ruby in pencil. The old hound had been napping, her expression one of complete contentment.

"I'll keep this always!" Nelle gave her brother a quick kiss.

"So that's what you're always scribbling when you're supposed to be doing your homework," their momma teased. Lewis grinned.

"You know I got my grades up this year, Momma!" he protested. "I studied lots!"

Pheen's gift was a square flat box. Nelle tore it open to reveal a diary with roses on the cover and a tiny golden key inserted into the lock.

"So you can keep Virgie from trying to read your private thoughts," Pheen laughed as Virgie frowned.

The last gift was a large, flat box. Tears filled Nelle's eyes as she opened it. She jumped up and ran to her mother.

"Momma!" She choked out, "you shouldn't have!"

In the box, nestled in tissue paper was the blue dress Nelle had borrowed for the dance contest.

Nan laughed and threw a look at her husband, who grinned.

"John's promised me a new dress for Christmas," she told them. "And you looked so pretty in it, Nelle. All grown up!"

"Can we have cake and ice cream now?" Virgie complained. "I'm hungry!"

Nelle and Pheen sat on the featherbed in the summer bedroom. The house was quiet, everyone else abed or getting ready for bed.

"Thanks for the diary! This has been just about the most perfect birthday ever!" Nelle giggled. "I almost wish I could turn sixteen again next year!"

Pheen yawned and Nelle pushed at her leg with her foot.

"Get on to bed yourself! I'm going to write my first entry in this diary. In private," she pointed her pencil at her sister, "if you don't mind?"

"I can take a hint!" Pheen rolled off the bed. "'Night, Nelle!"

Moonlight flooded the room Pheen shared with Virgie. She turned over and then turned back again, flipping her pillow over so that her cheek rested on the cool side. She couldn't stop thinking about the news. Near the end of May an American ship had been sunk by a German U-boat and a few days later, President Roosevelt had declared a state of emergency. It sure seemed like they were getting closer and closer to going to war.

She was too old to slip downstairs and huddle by the side of her parent's bed, something she'd done on sleepless nights when she was younger than Virgie was now. Her momma seemed to have a sixth sense where her children were concerned, for she'd always wake up and comfort Pheen, before guiding her gently back to her own bed. Her bed she'd shared with Nelle before Virgie got too old for a crib.

Pheen sat up. Sleep was farther away now than when she'd first lain down. Thoughts of war scared her. Who knew what would happen to her family if war came. Would George run off to Canada? Would her cousins join up? Or be drafted whether they wanted to go or not? She threw the sheet off and stood up. She slipped out of her room, careful not to wake Virgie, and crept down the hallway. Maybe Nelle would let her crawl in with her for what was left of the night.

The screen door to the summer bedroom made no sound as Pheen eased it open. In the moonlight, she could make out the mounded form of her sister, her back to the door.

"Nelle? Can I sleep with you?" Pheen whispered. "Nelle, can I?"

She pulled back the sheet and quilt and slipped into bed when Nelle didn't answer. Nelle made no sound as Pheen lay down. And after a few minutes, it came to Pheen that her sister was too still, no soft breathing sounded in the quiet of the night.

"Nelle? Nelle!" Alarmed, Pheen grabbed her sister's shoulder. Her hand closed on the plumpness of a feather pillow, not flesh. Jerking the covers back, Pheen stared aghast at the row of pillows that had fooled her into thinking her sister lay sleeping in her bed.

Where was Nelle?

CHAPTER TEN

Creeping back to her room, Pheen lay sleepless. She could guess where Nelle had gone. Or rather, if not exactly where, at least with whom. Hobart. And if their daddy found out that his daughter had sneaked out in the middle of the night, Nelle would be in big trouble and Hobart was likely to get more than an earful. She turned on her side and stared into the darkness. Should she have waited in Nelle's room—to let her sister know that her ruse had been discovered and to confront her? Wake their parents and let them know that Nelle was gone?

Dawn hadn't come yet when a soft footfall on the landing outside her bedroom told her that Nelle had returned. Breathing a sigh of relief, Pheen debated following her sister to the summer bedroom. Maybe, she considered, it would be better to let Nelle think no one had noticed that she'd slipped out. Then a thought struck her. Was this really the first time Nelle had sneaked away to meet Hobart? Or the first time that someone had caught her?

Although Pheen spent the next two weeks lying awake until the wee hours of the morning, Nelle didn't sneak out again.

"Child, are you taking sick?" Grandma Lavinia laid a hand across Pheen's forehead.

"No, Grandma," she answered, "I'm just worried." It was mid-July and the two—the old woman and her granddaughter—were shelling peas on the shaded back porch.

"What's got you so worried? That sister of yours?"

Pheen gave her grandmother a quick look. What did Grandma Lavinia know?

"Oh, no! Virgie's a pest sometimes, but she's got somebody to play with now that those little Pfyffe girls live down the creek. You know, at the old Jordan place."

Her grandmother chuckled.

"It weren't Virgie I was meaning. What's got you worried?"

"The news is something awful and it just keeps getting worse." Pheen burst out, dropping a handful of peas into her lap. "Most of the world is fighting, it seems like. Germany invading Russia!" She gulped. "Daddy says it's nothing to us. But he sure looks worried."

Her grandmother nodded.

"He does, that's the truth. But," she added, "he won't be drafted if war comes, Pheen. He'll be too old most like. And he'll be needed as a farmer."

"I wish I could be more like Nelle." Pheen dropped a pea husk onto the pile and picked up another pea pod. "She's always sure about everything. She's not worried at all."

"Wouldn't be too sure about that, if I were you." Grandma Lavinia met Pheen's gaze. "Some folks're just better at hiding their worries."

Carrying a jug filled with ice and lemonade in one hand and a stack of jewel-colored aluminum tumblers in the other, Pheen picked her way with care through the hay stubble. Ahead of her, Nelle drove the tractor down the field with Lewis and George on the hay wagon she pulled. Her daddy, along with Frank and Harry, threw hay bales onto the wagon for her brothers to stack. Pheen turned her face to the sun and winced. The July weather was plenty hot and dry—no rain in sight for this day at least. Nelle saw her sister coming and waved, stopping the tractor.

Handing about the cups to eager hands, Pheen filled each to the brim. Her cousins and her daddy squatted in the shade of the hay wagon. George and Lewis sat at the end of the wagon, leaning back against the stacked bales, legs dangling over the edge. Nelle climbed off the tractor, fanning herself with the battered straw hat she wore. She drank half her cup of lemonade with her eyes closed.

"Thank you!" Her daddy smiled at Pheen, pulling a faded blue bandana from his back pocket to wipe the sweat from his face and neck. "Looks like we'll get this field done before dark the way George keeps this old tractor running. Hasn't broke down once today."

"We get this hay in, Uncle John, maybe we can borrow George to look at Grandpa Millard's tractor." Frank pitched a pebble at George, who batted it away.

"That old tractor's always quitting right in the middle of work," Harry added. "Takes twice as long to get anything done on the farm."

"Sure," George told his cousins, "as long as it's okay with Daddy."

Frank pitched another pebble in Nelle's direction.

"What'dya think, Nelle?" he teased. "George gets that old thing running, you gonna come drive it for us?"

"Shucks, Nelle's a better driver than you!" Harry laughed. "She keeps her mind on the job, not like you, dear brother!" Harry drank off his lemonade and held out his cup for more. "We all know where your head is!"

George snickered and mouthed at Frank, "Julia Smith."

Frank threw a dirt clod at George and grinned at Nelle.

"That right, Nelle?"

"Sure do," she finished her lemonade, handed her tumbler to Pheen, and climbed back onto the tractor seat. Pheen noticed how her sister's hand cradled the ring hidden beneath her shirt. She'd bet a nickel Nelle's thoughts weren't all on driving the tractor.

"Let's get on with it." John Keller stood up and handed his cup to Pheen. "If you would, bring out a jug of ice water and a dipper. Leave it over yonder, under that tree by the hay barn."

"Aww, no!" George sat up and howled, clutching his head. "I can't believe it! DiMaggio's streak has ended!"

Grandma Lavinia shook her head and sighed, marking the page in her bible with a finger.

"Lordy, that young man had a good run!"

"But, the Indians!" George was beside himself. "Cleveland! I can hardly believe it!"

Nelle looked up from her magazine. "Who cares? It's just a stupid baseball game!"

"I bet Hobart cares!" George flung at her.

"Shut up, George!" Nelle bit off each word.

"Now there's no need for that kind of talk, young lady!" Nan Keller admonished her eldest. She motioned with a hand to the radio. "George, put some music on that we can enjoy. I don't want to hear any more news tonight."

Grumbling under his breath, George did as he was told. He made a face at Nelle, but she turned another page in the magazine and ignored him.

Pheen sat curled up in the corner of the couch, a book on her lap, her thoughts dulled. She was tired, tired to the bone from the stretch of hot July days and nights they'd been having. She wanted to go to bed, but the upstairs bedrooms were even hotter and no breeze came to cool the night down. It occurred to her to wonder where her daddy had gone. He'd left right after supper and a quick word to Momma.

"Where'd Daddy go?" George must have been wondering the same thing. "Wait'll he hears the news about Joe!"

"Nobody cares about some old baseball player but you," Nelle yawned.

"You don't know nothing about it. Mind your own business!" George retorted.

"One more word out of either of you," Nan Keller pointed at finger at Nelle then George, "and you are both going straight to your beds. I don't want to hear another word. I mean it!"

"Sorry, Momma!" Nelle and George spoke at once. Nan Keller rarely lost her temper and both cast a guilty glance at the other.

Pheen turned to her mother.

"Daddy's home!" The lights of the car shone through the window as it turned into the drive.

A few moments later, his footsteps could be heard on the kitchen porch.

"Get the door for me, George!" he called out.

Curious, Pheen straggled after George as he made for the screen door in the kitchen. The clank of glass bottles reached her as her momma came along behind her. John Keller set the wooden crate he carried on the sink countertop, handing a paper bag to his wife.

"Here you go," he grinned at her. "Ought to be enough there to cool ever'body down."

The crate held bottles of ice cold root beer and coke. Nan pulled a half-gallon of vanilla ice cream from the bag.

"Black Cows!" Nelle had crowded into the kitchen after her mother. "Mmm-mm! Thank you, Daddy!"

"I made a quick run to Blaine, before the store closed." He looked around. "Somebody wake Lewis and Virgie. And fix one of those for your grandma."

Pheen held a sweating bottle of root beer to her forehead, the glass cold against her skin, and closed her eyes. The snap of bottle caps being popped off bottles sounded as her daddy handed around the soda pops. She heard Virgie squeal with delight.

"Coke, please!" That was Lewis, as eager as they all were for the unexpected treat. She opened her eyes to meet her momma's smile as she handed out tall iced tea glasses filled with scoops of vanilla ice cream.

Sighs of appreciation sounded around the living room. For once, their momma allowed them to enjoy their floats with Grandma Lavinia. Soft music played on the radio, and quiet spurts of laughter erupted now and then. Pheen gazed around at the members of her family all gathered together and a sense of peace enveloped her. George and Nelle sat on the floor to either side of their grandma's rocking chair, for once not bickering. Virgie and Lewis were squashed together in the comfy armchair that normally Nelle would commandeer, both intent upon each bite of their Black Cows. Her parents sat at each end of the couch, while Pheen sat on the floor with her back against the couch near her momma. Tonight, all her worries receded and contentment washed over her. The world beyond this moment seemed far away.

The sweetness of that moment held as summer sped away, a new school year started, and snow covered hills and hollers alike before Thanksgiving. Hobart often drove Nelle home from school. If either of her parents noticed, no one said anything. The rides stopped early November and Nelle herself got quieter and quieter. The first week of December saw more snow, then a thaw, leaving the roads and hillsides slushy and muddy. Pheen sat cross-legged on her bed Saturday afternoon, her math book in her lap. Nelle stood looking out the front window, hugging herself.

"You cold?"

Nelle didn't answer for a moment, then she came to Pheen's bed, sat down and gathered up her cat, who'd been lying half under a throw on the bed.

"No, just thinking." She stroked her cat absently, his purr like a motor revving up beneath her hand.

"Thinking what?"

"Thinking I don't really need to finish high school."

"What?" Startled, Pheen dropped her pencil. Nelle shrugged.

"I'm not going to college, I'm going to get married. Hobart and I've talked about it. Soon as he can save enough money for a ring." She touched his class ring hidden under her sweater. "A real ring, not a going-steady ring. A for-keeps' ring!"

"Married!" Pheen clasped her hands together. "Married!" she repeated.

Nelle laughed.

"Don't look so shocked! People get married all the time. We can wait a bit, though. Besides a ring, Hobart wants to maybe move somewhere he can get a better job."

"Like where? Move where? Ashland?" Pheen couldn't believe what she was hearing. "You're only sixteen!

"Oh, Pheen!" She took a deep breath. "After he gets out of the service. And I'll be seventeen when June rolls around."

"Hobart enlisted?!"

"He says he can learn a trade. Get a better job," she shrugged. "And it's not like we're at war. But," her mouth set, she continued, "he better think again before he takes off from me."

"Momma! Daddy!" George's voice was frantic. Pheen stuck her head out her bedroom door. They'd gotten home from church and she was changing clothes before heading downstairs to help with Sunday dinner. What the dickens was wrong with her brother?

"The Japanese have attacked Pearl Harbor! It's on the radio! Pearl Harbor's been bombed!"

"Hush!" That was her daddy. "Be quiet, George! Let me listen!"

Nelle pushed Pheen out the way and clattered down the stairs with Pheen on her heels.

The voice from the radio repeated the news. Pheen felt fear blossom inside and looked to her sister. Nelle was clutching Hobart's class ring like a lifeline.

CHAPTER ELEVEN
1941-1942

Frank and Harry enlisted in the Army less than a week after Pearl Harbor, a day after America declared war on Germany and Italy. President Roosevelt had declared war on Japan the day after Pearl Harbor. Pheen found it hard to concentrate on schoolwork. Christmas came and went for her without the usual joy and merriment, although her momma and Grandma Lavinia went all out to make Christmas dinner a feast for eyes and stomach.

A roasted turkey and a cured ham held prominent positions at each end of the dining room table. Mashed potatoes with pools of melted butter, baked sweet potatoes, canned corn and beans, pickled beets, coleslaw, turkey dressing, two boats of gravy, and a mound of biscuits filled the center of the table. The old sideboard, polished until it glowed, held a coconut cake decorated with green and red sugars, and tins of shortbread, fudge, and divinity, as well as what Lewis and George hadn't eaten of the peanut brittle. A shallow wooden bowl held a pyramid of popcorn balls, while a cutglass basket sparkled in the light, bursting with plump red grapes and oranges.

The couch in the living room was moved away from the front window to make room for a Christmas tree. Fragile ornaments were brought out of storage and hung with care by Grandma Lavinia, Virgie, and Nelle. Nan made a pot of hot chocolate for the tree-trimming and passed around a box of festive Danish butter cookies. The radio was tuned to Christmas carols and John Keller placed the golden star atop the tree.

Nelle, except for coming out to help decorate the tree, spent hours in the upstairs bedroom, the door locked against unauthorized intrusions by Virgie. The whir of the sewing machine could be heard at intervals, and Virgie was sick with excitement over what Nelle might be doing. Pheen, privy to at least part of her older sister's activities, knew their little sister would be thrilled when she saw what Nelle had created. And in fact, it was the first time Pheen could ever remember that Virgie had nothing to say when she opened Nelle's gift. Speechless as she pulled out a beruffled dress of dark red velvet with white lace trim, she flung her arms around her oldest sister and burst into tears.

"It's beautiful! It's beautiful," she sobbed, while everyone else agreed. Tucked under it in the box was a nightgown made of sprigged white flannel, tiny ruffles on the bodice and at the ends of the sleeves, with pink ribbon sewn between the ruffles. Pheen thought it was the sweetest thing she'd ever seen. Nelle gave Lewis and George new comic books, her momma and Grandma Lavinia headscarves, and her daddy a tin filled with his favorite tobacco. Pheen received a leatherbound journal.

"To write down all your worries, so you don't have to carry them around with you," Nelle told her as she opened her gift.

By January of 1942, the first American troops arrived in Britain, and Frank and Harry were inducted and sent off to boot camp in New Jersey. Pheen kept a close eye on George—he'd be sixteen in the fall, but she didn't put it past him to lie about his age to the Army recruiter in Louisa. Nelle didn't say much. She still hadn't told her parents that she was going steady with Hobart, although they couldn't help but notice the letters that came weekly for her. Every night, Pheen wrote in her journal. *Please God keep Frank and Harry safe. Please let this war end soon.* These exact words or variations thereof started every entry she made. Grades, catty girls in the cafeteria, the weather—none of these mattered now. It was as if, she thought, she could keep her loved ones safe by repeating her prayers over and over.

Nelle stood in front of the window in the living room, next to her momma's lovebirds, reading the latest letter from Hobart. The birds were chirping and swinging together. As Pheen came into the room, Nelle sank down onto the couch. She answered Pheen's unspoken question, gesturing at the letter she clutched in her hand.

"Well, he's happy now!" Her voice was pitched low, filled with bitterness. "Wait and see if he doesn't get himself killed!"

Pheen went to her sister and sat beside her.

"Why? What's happened?"

"He got what he wanted—Hobart's on a ship now."

"In the Pacific?" America had sunk a Japanese destroyer—the Navy had recovered from Pearl Harbor and was fighting back now.

"No, he's on a ship protecting troop convoys." She waved the letter at Pheen. "On their way to Europe, he says."

"So, no fighting," Pheen reassured her sister.

"Sure, it's not like the Germans haven't been torpedoing ships!" Angry tears started in Nelle's eyes. "He didn't have to go and volunteer. He could've stayed here and … and," she took a deep breath. "We were going to make a good life together," she whispered.

Pheen held her sister close. It was like Hobart, she reflected. Lord knew she didn't wish any harm to him, but Hobart always did what Hobart wanted. She just wished he'd have left Nelle out of his plans.

Nelle sat up, sniffed, wiped her eyes.

"I have plans, too, and he better not forget it."

The winter eased into March and Nelle seemed in better spirits, as far as Pheen could tell. Her sister had taken in alterations in spite of her previous declaration that she'd never sew for uppity women. Everyone was making do with last season's clothes, but Nelle had a knack for updating them with trims and adjustments to sleeves, taking in seams in the bust or back to slim a profile, or alter collars and lapels to mimic the latest fashions. The sewing machine was in constant use after school and on the weekends. The money she earned was stuffed into the wooden box George had given her for Christmas. And with every dollar that went into the box, Nelle's disposition improved.

"Oh, Lizzie was fit to be tied!" Mae confided at lunch one afternoon. "Helen had Nelle alter that suit that Lizzie outgrew. Lizzie gave it to Helen, knowing it wouldn't fit right!" Mae shrugged. "She's my sister, but sometimes she can be spiteful."

And you should know, Pheen thought but didn't say. She'd been witness to many a spiteful comment Lizzie'd made to Mae—especially after Mae discovered people liked her and boys would invite her to dances and the movies. Still, who was she to call someone spiteful, Pheen chastised herself. She didn't get asked out either, but then, she didn't care. Who'd look twice at her with someone like Nelle in front of them?

"Have you heard from Hobart?" Pheen wondered.

"He writes to Momma. Says he might get shore leave soon, early April." Mae sighed. "Momma's worried to death about him, but I don't think Daddy'll take her to Norfolk to see him."

"Nelle?" Pheen stood outside her bedroom door and rattled the doorknob. "Nelle! Let me in!"

"Just a minute!" came a mumbled reply.

Pheen heard the lock click after a pause and shoved the door open. Nelle was sitting on her bed, bobby pins jutting from her mouth, and an old mirror propped against the headboard as she did up her freshly washed hair in pincurls.

"Why on earth did you lock the door?"

Nelle rolled her eyes, twisted the last strand of hair into a tight curl, and secured it with two pins. Surveying her work in the mirror, she wrapped a headscarf around her head and tied it on top of her head before answering.

"Virgie's always barging in." She yawned. "I wanted to get my hair set without her pestering me." She got up and took the mirror off the bed, leaning it against the wall by the door.

"Virgie's busy." Pheen perched on the end of her own bed. "Momma's seeing that she gets her homework done before her bath and bedtime. For once."

Nelle sat on the edge of her bed again. "I thought you were busy studying for that big math test tomorrow?"

"Finished for the night. I came up to see if my skirt needs ironing. The one I'm gonna wear to school tomorrow." She moved towards the clothes press she shared with her sisters.

Nelle slid off the far side of her bed, between Pheen and the clothes press.

"Look, Pheen," she gestured at the sewing machine. "I've already got the ironing board and iron set up. For all that sewing I've been doing." She turned Pheen toward the door. "If you'll carry that mirror downstairs to the storage room, I'll press your skirt and you can wear that sweater of mine that looks so good with it."

"Your navy sweater? For sure?"

Nelle smiled.

"Yep." She gave Pheen a small push. "Go on, before I change my mind."

The next morning, Lewis was coughing at breakfast, while Virgie picked at her food.

"Momma, my throat hurts when I swallow."

"Open your mouth and let me see," Nan instructed her, automatically placing a hand on her youngest daughter's forehead.

"Feels like you've got a bit of a fever." She turned to her mother-in-law. "Lavinia, would you fetch the bottle of aspirin from the medicine cabinet?"

"Yes, Lordy," Grandma Lavinia had stopped to rest her palm against Lewis' forehead. "Looks like we got two sick young'uns this morning."

Lewis whooped. "Does that mean I get to stay home from school?"

Nan dropped a kiss on top of his head as she took the bottle of aspirin from his grandmother and shook out a couple of pills.

"Yes, young man. Now swallow this." She handed him an aspirin before administering one to his sister.

"You go on and lie down on the couch," his grandmother told him. "I'll make you some hot lemonade and honey to sooth that cough."

"I'm sick, too, Grandma," Virgie protested.

"Of course you are," her mother smoothed her daughter's hair away from her face. "We'll put you in Momma and Daddy's big bed so you can rest downstairs."

Virgie turned to Nelle.

"Carry me, Nelle. I'm sick!"

Nelle pushed her chair away from Virgie.

"Stay away from me if you're sick! You can walk."

"That's right," Nan steered Virgie in the direction of the living room. "We'll get you settled in bed and bring you a hot drink to make your throat feel better."

Grandma Lavinia paused in the dining room with Lewis' drink. "Trust them both to get a cold at the same time!"

"You think that's all it is, Grandma?" Nelle sounded worried.

"Most likely. It's this changing weather, the first of April. Always brings on colds." She halted at the door into the living room. "You girls better get going, George's already got the car started."

Nelle grabbed her coat and her books, giving her grandma a hard hug before heading for the door.

"Don't forget, it's Friday. Momma said I could spend the night at Jenny's."

As the sisters hurried to the car, Pheen tugged at Nelle's arm.

"You haven't brought any overnight things."

Nelle slid into the front seat as Pheen climbed into the back.

"I already put my stuff in the trunk." She laughed. "So nice of Daddy to let us use the car instead of George's old truck."

"Hey!" George backed out onto the lane and drove towards the bridge that crossed Brushy Fork Creek. "Daddy needs the truck to deliver a load of lumber. He won't be back until late." The car rattled across the wooden planks of the bridge. "I told you yesterday."

By late Saturday afternoon, Nelle had not returned home from Louisa. At five o'clock, Nan turned to Pheen.

"You help your grandma see to Lewis and Virgie." She was pulling on her coat as she spoke. "Tell your daddy when he gets back from Paintsville that I've gone over to Blaine to use the phone at Mr. O'Bryant's store." She grabbed her purse and the keys to the car from the buffet. "I'm going to call Mrs. Pack and see what's keeping Nelle."

CHAPTER TWELVE
1942

Pheen and George sat side by side on the upper reaches of the stairs, eyes wide, eavesdropping as John Keller paced back and forth, listening to his wife.

"Molly Pack says Jenny was gone for the night on Friday, staying with her cousins over at Ulysses." They heard the rocker creak as their momma sat down. "Jenny came home as I was speaking with her mother. She said Nelle wasn't invited to spend the night in Louisa, and she didn't come to Ulysses with Jenny either."

Pheen couldn't take any more. She ran up the stairs into her room and looked about as if she could make Nelle appear by wishing her sister home. Where was Nelle? Slowly she touched her sister's bed, then went to the clothes press. She opened it and stood there for a moment before realizing what she was seeing. Empty hangers. Where Nelle's clothes should have hung. The suits she'd made for school. The blue dress their momma had given her. Standing on tiptoe, pushing aside the scarves and belts that lay on the top shelf, she reached for the polished wooden box George had given Nelle.

With trembling fingers, she opened the box. All the money Nelle had made from her alterations was gone. A single folded sheet of paper lay inside. On the outside was scrawled *To Momma and Daddy* in Nelle's handwriting. Pheen shut the box hard and swallowed. On impulse, she got down on her hands and knees and looked under her bed. The old suitcase that was stored there was gone. And it came to her, Nelle telling her how she'd already put her overnight things in the trunk of the car before school.

Her momma and daddy were in the kitchen, supper forgotten on the table, cups of coffee going cold before them, as Pheen walked in. Wordlessly, she handed the box to her momma.

Nan unfolded the sheet of paper and read it out loud.

Momma and Daddy, I'm taking the train from Louisa to North Carolina after school on Friday. Hobart's on leave, he's going to meet my train and we're going to get married soon's I get there. I'm sorry to sneak away this way, but it's the only chance we'll have for who knows how long with this war going on. I'll write when I have an address for you. I love you all. P.S. Please forgive me—Jenny didn't know anything about this, don't blame her. I knew you wouldn't let me go, but my mind was made up. Nelle

John groaned and placed his head in his hands. Tears rolled down Nan's cheeks. Pheen thought her heart would burst.

"Dammit!" Her daddy took the paper from her momma and read it again. "She's too young to get married! I have half a mind to go after her." The paper crumpled in his fist. "That Hobart! If I had a hold of him, I'd...."

"She'll be seventeen in two months," Nan reflected and wiped the tears from her eyes. She looked to Pheen.

"You didn't know about this?"

"No, Momma, she never said a word." Taking a deep breath, Pheen reported the rest of her news. "Her clothes are gone, she took that suitcase."

Later, lying in her bed, the lights out, the house quiet, she thought back to Nelle working so hard on all those alterations, grinning as her wooden box filled with money. Of the night before Nelle had gone, her sister offering to iron her skirt so she wouldn't open the clothes press. She must have locked the door to pack her things, then slid the suitcase back under the bed. And the next morning, with everyone fussing over Lewis and Virgie, there'd been plenty of time to stow the suitcase in the trunk of the car. And to take it out after school before anyone saw her. Pheen turned over on her side, away from Virgie's bed, and cried herself to sleep.

Half the girls at school were agog with the news of Nelle's elopement. Pheen heard the whispers as she walked from class to class.

"Married!" That was Jenny Pack and her cousins. "My parents are watching me like a hawk now! I can't go anywhere without my brother Jerry tagging along. And," she heaved a huge sigh, "I've got the earliest curfew I've had since I was in junior high!"

"I bet she got 'married'!" That was Helen in the cafeteria, Lucille and all the other girls at her table sniggering except for Lizzie. Hobart's oldest sister looked like she'd swallowed a lemon, her face puckered and red.

Mae plopped her tray down by Pheen and pulled up a chair. She glanced over at the table of senior girls.

"Don't listen to any of them, Pheen." She patted Pheen's hand and leaned in close. "Momma's had a letter from Hobart. He sent a clipping from the local paper there in North Carolina. He and Nelle are definitely married." She shivered, then brightened. "That makes you and me as good as sisters!"

Pheen tried to smile. "I bet your parents weren't too happy with the news."

Mae looked uncomfortable. "Well, I think they wished he'd waited. Nelle's awfully young!"

Pheen took a bite of her sandwich and didn't answer. Everyone knew how stuck up those Arnetts were—excepting Mae, of course. She'd bet more than a nickel that Hobart's parents weren't at all happy that he'd married Nelle Keller.

Mae finished her lunch.

"Have you heard from Nelle?"

Pheen shook her head. Not yet. Not a word. She missed her sister so much it made her heart ache. Nelle's movie magazines were stacked in the living room next to the chair where she'd sit reading. A package of bubblegum lay discarded on the mantel in the dining room. Bobby pins were scattered across the bureau in their bedroom. Virgie, even in the warmth of June, refused to wear anything but her flannel nightgown to bed each night, hugging it as if hugging her sister. Some nights, Pheen sat with her little sister, rubbing her back, until she fell asleep. Lewis didn't say much, but stuck to George like glue—as if afraid his older brother might go missing one day. And George—he drove himself and Pheen to school each day still and twice came home with dusty clothes, once with a bloody lip, after calling out any boy who dared say a word against Nelle. To mention Hobart's name was to get a fierce glare in return, warning whoever said his name to back off.

The first letter from Nelle arrived shortly after her seventeenth birthday, addressed to her momma.

> *Dear Momma, I promised to write you, so here goes. I'm living in a rooming house here in North Carolina, near where Hobart and I got married. It's as close as I can get to the naval base at Norfolk, housing is really hard to find. Most of the other girls who live here are close in age and are also married, so I have someone to talk to. Mrs. Porter is our landlady and we pay her for room and board. Don't worry, she's a good cook and the house is very clean! 'War brides' is what the government calls us and they give us twenty dollars a month allotment, so I can afford to stay here okay. When his ship comes back to port, Hobart and I hope to have some time together.*
>
> *Don't think that I don't miss you all! I do, but my place is here now that I'm a married woman. Please give Lewis and Virgie and Grandma a hug for me. Tell Pheen to write me and tell George I miss him too even though I know he's probably mad at me. And tell my daddy not to be mad at me either.*
>
> *Love you all, Nelle*

Pheen wrote once a week to her sister, passing on what news she heard, *"Frank and Harry came home on leave last week, they wouldn't say where they'll be going,"* tales from home, *"Virgie insisted on opening your summer bedroom, but she didn't last one night out there alone*." She didn't tell Nelle that she couldn't bring herself to sleep in the summer bedroom, even though it would be cooler. When school started again, she passed on stories of the usual goings-on—who was going steady with whom, who'd broken up, going to the movies with George and Mae. She didn't tell her either how she and George weren't sure they'd be able to keep attending high school—not with gasoline being rationed the way it was. Their daddy needed those coupons for his timber sales.

Near the end of October, Frank and Harry were aboard ship heading across the Atlantic—destination unknown. George listened to the nightly news without fail, as intent as his grandmother. He kept the old truck and the car in topnotch condition—coaxing every mile possible from a gallon of gas. Rather than drop out of school, the principal allowed them to come in two days a week and do the rest of their work at home. They worked together in the dining room after supper was over, encouraging each other. George was determined to do well, to graduate early, and although he never mentioned it, Pheen knew that he was counting down to his eighteenth birthday. If the war was still going on then, he'd be able to enlist without his parents' permission.

One night, after finishing their homework, George closed his math book with a grunt. The radio in the living room was tuned to the Abbott and Costello weekly show. Grandma Lavinia could be heard chuckling at the duo's routine.

"I'd enlist next fall," he told his sister in a low voice. "It sure looks like this war's not ending anytime soon." He rubbed a hand over his eyes. "But after Nelle sneaked off the way she did, I can't do that to Momma and

Daddy." His voice dropped to a whisper. "After she was gone, I saw him—Daddy—in the barn, crying where he thought no one would see him."

Pheen bit her lip and reached out to squeeze her brother's hand.

Just then, Lewis came in, a small square of paper in his hand.

"Pheen, this is for Nelle. Send it with your letter this week, okay?"

He'd drawn Nelle's cat, the tom curled up on Nelle's bed.

"I surely will, Lewis. She's gonna love it!"

Her little brother, squeaky clean after his bath and ready for bed, gave Pheen a quick hug and darted away. But not before she saw his mouth quiver and tears form in his eyes. They all missed Nelle.

Dear Pheen, be sure and tell Lewis that I love the drawings he sends me. I take them out and look at them whenever I get too homesick, but don't tell Momma or Daddy I said that! Hobart's ship has been in port a couple of times. I don't always get to see him—he's part of the maintenance crew so sometimes he doesn't get more than a couple hours of shore leave. But he always calls me so I know he's okay. He says there's talk the ship might come out of active service and be used for training. I'm praying he's right! It would mean we'd be together—be able to find a house and make a real home together.

The holidays were subdued. Grandma Lavinia and Nan saved up enough sugar coupons to be able to do some baking, they bartered a small ham for a turkey from their neighbors—the Jordans, and George and Lewis took Virgie up on the ridge behind the farm to pick out a Christmas tree. Nelle sent them all small gifts and Pheen knew that her parents had sent a package to Nelle, but Christmas wasn't the same without her big sister. Nelle had always been there. It was with a sense of relief that the New Year approached.

CHAPTER THIRTEEN
1943

"Don't be getting any ideas, George!" John Keller addressed his eldest son. It was after supper, the family gathered in the living room. Lewis lay on the floor, drawing, while Virgie was curled up on the couch with her head in her mother's lap. Their daddy was hunched over on the end of the couch, listening to the news. Pheen sat in the rocker, her grandmother having gone to bed early. George, sitting in the armchair with his history book open on his lap, looked up.

"What? What's going on?"

"Joe DiMaggio enlisted in the Army today!" Lewis piped up.

"I'm not old enough to enlist!" George protested.

"All the same, don't you be thinking about it," his daddy cautioned, then sat back as the news ended.

Pheen thought her brother looked like he might have something else to say, but he turned the page in his history book and made another note on the pad next to his chair. She closed the journal she'd been writing in and stood up, yawning.

"I'm going to bed. G'night, Momma, Daddy."

In her bedroom, she lay in the dark. She might as well write to Nelle instead of in her journal. Her thoughts never strayed far from her sister—or how this horrible war had pulled them apart. Young men of age had either enlisted or been called up already. If the war dragged on another year, George would enlist and she'd have to face the chance of losing her brother. No more letters had come from Frank or Harry. It was awful not knowing if they were alive or dead, although no telegram had come to her aunt and uncle. How would it feel, she wondered, to have two sons off to war?

Things at home were getting harder—coffee had been rationed, gasoline still, store-bought bread and even shoes were now rationed! They were lucky, they could grow and can vegetables, raise their own livestock to butcher, grind chicory roots to make the coffee last longer—all the things they'd done in the past—the old ways not forgotten. But Nelle was living in town, where things would cost more and be harder to come by. No Grandma Lavinia to bake bread. Always, always, her thoughts returned to her sister. Maybe things would get better with the coming of spring. Pheen turned over and pulled her quilt over her head, willing herself to sleep, to forgetfulness.

Spring brought warm weather, but no relief from the war news. Rationing now included meat, butter, and cheese. Churchill came to America in mid-May for a meeting with President FDR, dashing Pheen's hopes that a sudden end to the war might be coming. Nelle's letters now were infrequent and short when they came.

> *Dear Momma, the heat is really getting to me here. It's been so sticky, I don't have the energy to do much of anything these days. And the food—well, Mrs. Porter tries, but she doesn't have much to go on with. I don't hardly have an appetite anyway. Hobart had a few days of shore leave a couple of months ago, but I have barely seen him since. Hope you are all doing good back home.*
> *Love to everybody, Nelle*

Pheen sighed with relief when she turned in her last English and history papers at the first of June. School was over early for the summer, and she was glad of it. She and George were on the front porch, George napping in the swing and Pheen curled up in one of the big wicker rockers, writing a letter that she hoped would reach Nelle in time for her birthday. Eighteen! Nelle was turning eighteen in just a few days. A cloud of dust could be seen where a car was coming along the lane towards the bridge that crossed the creek. As it crossed the bridge, Pheen saw *Stidham's Taxi Service* on the door. The car slowed as it passed their house. Turning in at their drive, it pulled up to the side gate and stopped. The driver got out and hurried around to the passenger door. As the passenger door swung open, Pheen leaped to her feet.

"Nelle! It's Nelle!" she cried. "Nelle's home!"

George jerked awake, half sat up, and fell out of the swing as he tried to roll over and stand up at the same time. Pheen reached the gate, throwing her arms around her sister. Nelle clung to Pheen, both of them crying. And then her momma was there and Pheen let go as Nelle threw herself into her mother's arms. Lewis, she saw, was going at a run across the field towards the barn to get their daddy. Grandma Lavinia stood on the front porch, Virgie beside her, her face buried on her grandmother's shoulder as she sobbed.

Nelle sat at the kitchen table, a glass of cold water before her. Pheen thought she looked tired, with dark circles under her eyes. Her golden blonde hair seemed dulled, its shine dimmed.

"Lordy, child," their grandmother fussed about, setting a loaf of bread, butter, and a pot of jam on the table. "Why didn't you let us know you were coming?"

"I wanted to see Hobart before I came home. After he went back to his ship, I got my ticket and here I am." She pushed the food away. "I know I just got here, but if I could lie down for a bit?"

Her grandmother exchanged a glance with Nan.

"Honey, you go right in my bedroom there off the dining room. John's put a fan in there for me, it'll be cooler than you going upstairs."

Nan shook her head when George bent to pick up his sister's suitcase. "Leave it."

"I was going to take it upstairs to the summer bedroom." George looked from his momma to his grandmother.

"You can see to it later."

Pheen hovered at the foot of the bed as her mother slipped Nelle's shoes off and coaxed her to lie down. Grandma Lavinia came in with a glass of water and another glass of ice chips. Worried, Pheen adjusted the fan so it played across the bed. Was Nelle sick? Was that why she'd come home?

Nan sat on the edge of the bed and took Nelle by the hand.

"How far along are you, honey?"

"Two months, I reckon."

"You sick mornings?" Grandma Lavinia pointed at the bedside table. "Suck on those ice chips if you start feeling nauseous. I'll make you some ginger tea." She bustled from the room.

"It'll soon pass, the sickness," Nan reassured her eldest daughter. "Another month at the most. I'll bring you some saltines to nibble on if you feel like it."

Alone with her sister, Pheen gingerly sat on the bed next to Nelle.

"A baby?"

Nelle nodded.

"Yes, due this December." She watched the door. "I didn't mean to come home, either. Hobart insisted, said he'd feel better me being here with my momma." Her mouth set in a straight line. "But soon's I have this baby, we are leaving here. I don't care what Hobart says."

The news spread quickly that Nelle was home and pregnant. At the movies in Louisa with George in late July, Pheen's ears burned as the gossip washed over her.

"Pregnant?" That was Helen Prater in the seat behind her, along with Lucille and Lizzie. Mae was nowhere to be seen. "Probably lying," Helen suggested with a snort. "Probably lying about being married, too!"

"Just another Allotment Annie," Lucille declared, putting in her two cents' worth. "No telling how many sailors she's married to get those allotments for wives!"

"Oh, she married Hobart all right," Lizzie acknowledged, ripping the wrapper off a candy bar. "He sent Mama a newspaper clipping right after he married her." Lizzie sniffed. "I had to get the smelling salts for poor Mama, she took the news that hard!"

Pheen stiffened, one more word out of those three! George's hand clamped on her shoulder.

"Don't pay those harpies no mind! Spiteful biddies, all of them," he whispered.

Helen had the last word. "Well, it looks like you'll be 'Aunt' Lizzie soon!" She and Lucille chortled with laughter at that, then pounded Lizzie on the back as she coughed and choked on the last bite of her Mars bar.

"Hey, y'all! Hush!" The moviegoers around the trio vented their displeasure and the hateful whispers stopped.

Nelle shrugged after one look at Pheen's face.

"I don't care what they say." She bit off the corner of a saltine cracker and shivered as she swallowed it. "I told you a long time ago to ignore those girls." Putting down the cracker with a grimace, she lay a hand on her belly. "I'm married to Hobart, and I'm having his baby, whether they believe it or not."

She lay back on her grandmother's bed and swung her feet up.

"I'm tired, Pheen. I'm going to sleep for a bit." A yawn escaped her. "Close the door, would you, on your way out."

Pheen did as she was told. Nelle had remained in her grandmother's bedroom, keeping her downstairs close to the bathroom. Her grandmother slept on a cot set up in the dining room under the windows, declaring that it was perfectly comfortable and let her sleep near Nelle, should she need anything in the night. Later that evening, before going to bed herself, Pheen slipped downstairs for a glass of water. Halfway down the stairs, her parent's voices stopped her. The creaking of the rocking chair told her that her grandmother was still up as well.

"She don't eat more'n a bird, Nan," her father's anxious words carried clearly to her, although he kept his voice pitched low. So Nelle wouldn't hear, she figured. "That can't be good for her or that baby she's carrying."

"No," her momma agreed, "it's not. Another week or so, the morning sickness should ease. I'm hoping her appetite will be better then."

The rhythmic creak of the rocking chair stopped.

"That girl's worrying herself sick over something."

"What?" That was her daddy again. "What's worrying her? It's her first, you think that's it?"

"I don't rightly know," Grandma Lavinia said. "I don't think that's it. Any such worries, she could take to her momma or me."

Nan sighed. "I'll see if I can get her to talk to me tomorrow, John."

Pheen turned and went back to her bedroom.

If her momma ever learned what was worrying her eldest daughter, Pheen never heard. As her morning sickness ended, Nelle's appetite picked up. The garden's summer bounty helped, too, Pheen was sure. It seemed to her that their tomatoes had never been so juicy and flavorful, or the peas and beans and corn so tender. New potatoes simply boiled and slathered with butter churned from their own cows' milk filled heaping plates. Peaches and cherries came in, and apple and pears rounded on limbs heavy with fruit.

Mae came to visit one day, presenting a paper bag to Nelle with a shy smile. Nelle pulled out a small pieced quilt, done with calico fabrics in pale shades of blue and green, yellow and pink.

"Do you like it?" Mae watched Nelle stroking the fabrics. When she looked up, Nelle's eyes were bright with tears. She reached out to hug Mae. "It's beautiful! Did you make this yourself?"

Mae nodded, beaming.

"Daddy took me to Blaine to pick out the fabrics." She touched the quilt with a tentative finger. "He's excited to be a grandfather, Nelle."

Having heard Lizzie that day at the movies, Pheen felt certain that Mrs. Arnett was not looking forward to becoming a grandmother to Nelle's baby. Nelle and Hobart's baby, she corrected herself.

Nelle's appetite continued to be good throughout the fall, and her spirits seemed to improve as well. Grandma Lavinia busied herself crocheting baby booties and a blanket. John Keller carried the sewing machine down to his mother's bedroom. Nelle sewed nightgowns for the baby from delicate fabrics and laces her momma and grandmother produced from trunks. These also yielded some of Virgie's and Lewis' baby clothes, much to the delight of Virgie.

"I bet you have a girl! Wait and see, a girl like me!" she crowed.

Lewis' contribution to the baby's layette was a drawing of a kitten from a litter born in the barn and one of a puppy from a litter on the neighbor's farm.

"Babies for your baby, Nelle."

Nelle pulled them both—Virgie and Lewis—close for a tight hug, tears streaming down her face.

"I'm just a big old baby myself these days. I wish this child would hurry up and get here." She sighed. "We'll be a real family then—Hobart and me and our baby."

Her wish came true the first week of December, two weeks before the doctor had figured she was due. Her labor seemed to go on too long and Nan sent John for old

Doc Carter. Pheen had strict orders to keep Virgie and Lewis upstairs out of the way. George retreated to the shed where the old truck was housed and tinkered with the engine. Her daddy sat in the kitchen, a cup of coffee cold on the table before him. Leaving the younger ones in the bedroom with the door firmly closed, Pheen crept down to the foot of the stairs and listened. One loud, long moan from Nelle reached her, then total silence. She waited and waited, watching the clock on the mantel.

After three-quarters of an hour passed, Doc Carter came out of the bedroom with Grandma Lavinia. He paused in the kitchen, spoke a few words to her daddy, then shook his hand and left. John Keller buried his face in his hands, his shoulders shaking. Her grandma sat down beside her son, put her arm around him and leaned her head against him.

CHAPTER FOURTEEN
1944

Nancy Rose Arnett was buried the day after she was born, having lived less than an hour. *Hydrocephalous*, the death certificate read. Nan dressed her granddaughter in the finest of the garments Nelle had sewn and wrapped her in the blanket Grandma Lavinia had crocheted. With her body swathed in the blanket and her head hidden from view, Nancy Rose might have been a doll. Wisps of fine, blonde hair curled about the edges of the blanket and her eyes were blue, like Nelle's. Lewis and Virgie were allowed to see her before Nan placed the baby in her daughter's arms for the first and last time. Pheen and George paid their respects, then Grandma Lavinia shooed them away to give Nelle some privacy before the doll-like body was placed in a coffin and taken for burial in the family plot up on the ridgetop. John Keller dug the tiny grave himself.

The birth had been hard, and Nelle was not allowed out of bed to attend the funeral and burial. Hobart did not come home. Mae and her father joined Pheen's parents, Pheen, and her siblings on the cold, windswept ridgetop while the minister led them in prayers. Christmas, two weeks' later, was the saddest one that Pheen could ever remember. Nelle stayed in the bedroom with the shade drawn. Nan or Grandma Lavinia took her meals on a tray. She refused to see anyone else.

On the day after New Years,' Pheen came downstairs early to find Nelle up, dressed, and wearing her winter coat. She was rooting about in the top center drawer of the buffet.

"I need a stamp, Pheen," Nelle brandished a letter in her free hand. "I need to mail this right away." She poked a finger into the drawer. "Never mind, here's some stamps."

"You should sit down, Nelle," Pheen pulled out a chair from the dining table. "Here, sit."

"I don't have time to sit. Never mind then. Where's George?" She looked towards the living room and nodded at Pheen. "Go wake him up. I need to go into town."

Alarmed, Pheen shook her head.

"You can't go into town!"

"Go get George!" Nelle's voice rose to a screech. "Go get him!"

The kitchen door opened and their momma came in with a milk pail, Grandma Lavinia on her heels with a basket of eggs.

"Here, what's going on?" Nan Keller set the pail down on the sink counter in the kitchen with a thud and came into the dining room, taking in the sight of Nelle, fully dressed and face pale, but tight with anger. "Sit down, Nelle, before you fall down," she ordered.

Nelle sat. Her momma took her coat and headscarf off.

"You're in no condition to be going anywhere, honey," she told Nelle. "Anything you need or want, you just let us know. Your daddy and George're more than happy to run for you."

"What I need is to mail this letter and then send a telegram to Hobart." Nelle's chin came up. "He needs to know I'm coming soon's I get my ticket." Her bravado deflated and she lay her head in her arms on the table. Great sobs escaped as her shoulders heaved.

"Oh honey!" Nan knelt beside her daughter and took her into her arms. Grandma Lavinia slipped past them into the bedroom and straightened the sheet and quilts on the bed. Her momma jerked her head at Pheen to come help her. Together they got Nelle into the bedroom and out of her coat, and onto the bed. As Pheen started to leave, Nelle grabbed her hand.

"Don't go, Pheen!"

Nan pulled Grandma Lavinia's sewing rocker close to the bed and Pheen sat, holding her sister's hand. The tears had stopped and Nelle lay on her side, facing Pheen, her eyes closed. When Pheen was sure that Nelle was asleep, she tugged gently at her hand, but in the instant she did so, Nelle's fingers tightened on her own. Watching her sleep, Pheen felt like crying herself. Married, but with Hobart gone because of a war she'd never believed would come, then losing her first baby— she didn't know how a body could endure so much heartbreak. Nelle was just eighteen years old. Her grip tightened on the hand she held, and she settled herself to sit as long as Nelle needed her.

The sound of Grandma Lavinia hushing Virgie as dinner was ready made Pheen's stomach growl, but she stayed where she was. Low voices reached her from the kitchen, as dinner was served there instead of the dining room. The low rumble was her daddy, that answering murmur her momma. With a quick intake of breath, Nelle turned over on her back and let go of Pheen's hand. As Nelle pushed herself into a sitting position, Pheen jumped up to plump the pillows behind her back.

"I'm sorry I yelled at you this morning."

"That's okay," Pheen reassured her. "But Momma's right. You're not strong enough to go back to North Carolina."

Nelle blew out a deep breath.

"You might as well know, Pheen. Everybody will soon enough." She rubbed her hand across her eyes. "I'm going to California."

"California?"

Nelle was near tears again.

"I told y'all that Hobart's ship was coming out of service to be a training ship, remember?"

At Pheen's bewildered nod, she continued.

"Well, a bunch of the men asked for transfers to a new ship, so's they could be in the fighting."

"And Hobart was one of them?" Trust Hobart, she thought with a rush of anger. Married and with a baby on the way, he'd elected to leave Nelle behind to fend for herself. Nelle nodded.

"And the new ship, the USS Independence, is part of the Pacific fleet. So he's going to be in the middle of the war against the Japanese. Hobart's on shore leave this month, he's renting a little house in a place called Hollister with another guy from his ship." She drew a deep breath. "There's no way he's going to come back home to Kentucky on any leave he gets. So I'm going out there."

"California!" Pheen shook her head. "Stay here with us, Nelle. We'll take care of you!"

"You don't understand." Nelle was adamant. "That's what Hobart keeps saying, every letter I get from him. But he needs to remember that he's a married man now. And I plan to be that reminder."

Pheen didn't know what to say. Once Nelle made up her mind about something, no use arguing with her.

When Nelle spoke again, her voice was quiet.

"We fought all the time in North Carolina. He kept saying I should go back home." She looked away, as if reliving again those hours spent fighting. "I tried to tell him that my home was with him. In the end, I gave in. I was sick every single day and I was tired, I didn't want to fight no more."

She met her sister's gaze.

"But this time, he's not getting his way. I may have lost my baby, but I still have a husband. I'm going to California, whether Hobart likes it or not."

Her words echoed in Pheen's mind in the days which followed. *My baby*, Nelle had said. Not *our baby*. Did that mean Hobart hadn't wanted either Nelle or the baby in North Carolina?

"I'm going to California if I have to walk to Louisa to catch the train," Nelle insisted to her parents when they begged her not to leave. "I can pay for my ticket with money from my allotment checks."

"At least stay long enough to build up your strength," that was Grandma Lavinia's compromise.

"One more week is all." Nelle's face was drawn, but she didn't back down. "Hobart's on shore leave. I want to get to California before his leave ends." She took a deep breath. "The train trip isn't as long as you think, it's only two-three days, depending on stopovers. And this way, Hobart'll be able to meet my train."

Pheen and George went with their daddy to take Nelle to the train station. Nan and Grandma Lavinia said their good-byes at home, along with Lewis and Virgie. Virgie had to be pulled away from Nelle's skirts, where she clung, sobbing as Nelle tried to reassure her.

"Just think, Virgie, when I get all settled, you and Momma and Daddy and everybody can come to visit me in California! You'd like that!"

Virgie was still crying when the car crossed the bridge over Brushy Fork. While they waited for boarding to begin, John Keller admonished his daughter.

"Now Nelle, listen here. I want you to send us a telegram as soon as you get to California." He cleared his throat. "And here, here's a little something to see you on your way." He slipped some folded bills into her hand.

"I don't need any money, Daddy!" Nelle protested.

He closed her fingers over the folded dollar bills and cleared his throat again. Passengers began to board. "You never know what might happen. A long layover, something like that."

Nelle hugged him hard. Then it was Pheen's turn. She let go of Nelle reluctantly, stepping back as George hefted her suitcase. He cleared his throat much as his father had done.

"You tell Hobart Arnett he better be good to you, or he'll answer to me." He handed her up the steps into the train car.

"Write me!" Pheen called. "Write to me, Nelle!"

Nelle waved and disappeared into the train car.

Arrived safely. Hobart met my train. Will write and give you my address. Love to all. Nelle.

A week later the first letters came—one addressed to her parents and one to Pheen. Pheen carried the letter in her pocket to school the next day, where she could touch it—as if touching it could bring Nelle closer.

At lunchtime, she picked a table far away from her classmates and concentrated on her sandwich, the letter opened before her. When Mae pulled out a chair at the table, Pheen hastily folded up her letter and tucked it back in the envelope.

Mae watched her in silence for a moment, then took her sandwich from her lunch bag.

"You don't have to put your letter away," she told Pheen sadly. "Hobart's written to Momma about how Nelle's disobeyed him and come out to California."

Pheen snorted.

"He's not her daddy!"

"He shouldn't have gotten married if he didn't want a wife." Mae's next words surprised her. Her friend reached out to touch Pheen's hand. "I mean, if I was married, I'd want to be with my husband—especially if he was going to go off fighting in the war."

Pheen bit into her sandwich. That's what Nelle had said.

Dear Pheen, I don't know how I can love this man when all we do is fight every day. It's just like North Carolina all over again. Except I'm not pregnant this time and I'm not leaving and he can't seem to get that through his thick skull. Please don't tell Momma and Daddy though. I'm eating good and resting as much as I can. The house is small, but cute and it's my first real home with Hobart. His roommate moved out and that's another thing Hobart's mad about. Now he's got to pay all of the rent, instead of only half of it. I reminded him that I get twenty

*dollars a month and he can use that money to help
pay for rent if he needs it. If only he'd quit badgering
me to go back to Kentucky, sometimes I think he's
sorry he married me.*

*But there's two nice women who live to either side of
us—both married to sailors on Hobart's ship. Joan
and Betty have been real good to me—inviting me for
coffee and showing me where to shop for groceries
and such. If I need anything at all, they said to let
them know.*

*Well, I'll close for now. I'm not coming home any
time soon, no matter what Hobart wants.*

Your loving big sister,

    Nelle

CHAPTER FIFTEEN

No letters came from Nelle the last week of January. Instead, a telegram was delivered via *Stidham's Taxi Service* on February 1st. Pheen and George were in the driveway, getting in the car to leave for school when the taxi pulled in. George took the telegram and looked at Pheen, gulping.

"Daddy!" Pheen hollered. John Keller had just strode onto the drive from the pathway to the barn, a pail of milk in either hand. George waved the telegram. The milk pails sloshed as their daddy handed a pail to each of them and grabbed the telegram from George's hand.

"What is it, John? Is it Nelle? Is she coming home?" Hope flared on Nan's face. Grandma Lavinia turned from the sink where she was washing the breakfast dishes and watched as her son tore open the envelope.

His face drained of color as he read the telegram.

"Yes, she's coming home, our baby girl's coming home." He handed the telegram to his wife, who began to read it aloud.

" *'Regret to inform you there's been an accident.* Stop. *Nelle dead.* Stop. *Have arranged for her body to be sent home.* Stop. *Letter to follow.* Stop. *Hobart Arnett.'"*

The telegram crumpled in Nan's fingers as she collapsed onto a chair at the kitchen table. The glass Grandma Lavinia was holding slipped from her grasp and shattered on the linoleum. George's fingers bit into Pheen's shoulder, then he turned and disappeared outside. Pheen heard the car start before it roared off down the lane. She dropped her books on the floor, shut the door George had left open, and reached for the broom and dustpan to sweep up the broken glass.

She couldn't catch her breath. Virgie was bawling in her grandmother's arms. Pheen headed outside. Lewis was hunched up on the kitchen porch, his face buried in Ruby's neck. Pheen ran. At the path across the field, she turned towards the barn. The smell of warm cows greeted her, and old Jerse, their Jersey cow, lowed as Pheen hurried past her stall. At either end of the barn, on both sides of the wide center aisle, ladders led up to the haylofts above the stalls. Pheen climbed the ladder at the far end of the barn to the loft above where broken bales and loose hay formed a pile from which her daddy or George would feed the cows and Devil the bull. She burrowed into the loose hay, fists pressed to her eyes as tears fell. Sobs shook her body. Nelle, gone forever! How? How could it be possible?

Curling deeper into the hay, Pheen drifted in and out of a state of misery until at last she slept. George's frantic voice woke her.

"Josephine Joy? Pheen? You in here?"

She sat up as George's head popped up over the top of the ladder. His eyes were red and swollen.

"Momma and Daddy are worried sick." He turned his head away from her and wiped at his eyes. "Come on back to the house. Don't scare everybody by disappearing. Not now."

Hobart's letter arrived the following day, along with a copy of Nelle's death certificate. The letter said only that he'd been waking up, getting ready to leave for the base, when he found Nelle on the floor in the kitchen. Gas was leaking from the stove. It appeared she'd been preparing to make their breakfast. He was heartbroken that he hadn't found her in time to save her. And he was sorry, but the USS Independence was departing immediately for duty in the south Pacific—he wouldn't be coming home for her funeral.

The next day, Thursday, Nelle's coffin arrived in Louisa on the train and was collected from the station by the Childers and Sloane Funeral Parlor. Her trip home from California had only taken two days. Pheen rode into town to the funeral parlor with George and Grandma Lavinia in the old truck, while her parents took the car with Lewis and Virgie. Pheen was old enough to remember when Grandpa Keller had passed. The family had come into the funeral parlor then, too, for a private viewing. The casket had been half-opened, and she could see her grandfather lying there as if sleeping as they filed past and solemnly paid their respects.

Nelle's coffin wasn't open. It was completely sealed shut, but a flat viewing window was let into the lid of the casket. Her parents approached the casket together. Pheen watched as her momma cried out and buried her face in her hands. John Keller held his wife and stared unmoving for long moments at his eldest daughter. Then Grandma Lavinia approached with Virgie and Lewis. The old woman lay her hand on the window as if to stroke her granddaughter's cheek, then she led her youngest grandchildren away.

Pheen gulped. George was squeezing her hand so tightly, she thought her fingers might be pinched off. And there was Nelle—her beautiful, headstrong sister. Golden waves framed her face, and yes, she looked as if she might be sleeping. *Wake up, wake up*! Pheen wanted to scream, to pound her fists on that glass window until those eyes opened and the mouth smiled, until Nelle came back to them. George was muttering something under his breath, but she didn't catch his words. She turned away from the sight she couldn't bear to look at and saw her father hand off his wife to his mother. He approached the funeral director, young Mr. Sloane. John Keller gestured at the casket, led the director to it, pointed at Nelle, gesturing again at his daughter. She couldn't hear what the two men were saying. Mr. Sloane shook his head side to side, pointing at the casket. He shrugged, shook his head again. Her daddy's shoulders drooped, he went to Nan and put his arm around her.

"Let's go home."

"But, Daddy!" That was George, urgent.

"I said, let's go home. Now."

George went without another word. Pheen followed after the others, pausing for a last glance back at her sister. It seemed wrong, somehow, to go home and leave Nelle all alone.

"I tried, Nan," John Keller looked defeated. The family had made it into the kitchen when they got home, as if no one had the energy to go any farther into the house.

"But, Daddy," George wouldn't be hushed a second time. "They've got to open her casket! That towel! Why's there a towel wrapped around Nelle's neck like that? What's it hiding?" He couldn't sit still, jumping up and pounding his fist on the kitchen table. "He killed her! I know he did!"

"Now, George," his mother's voice was raw from crying. "You heard your father."

"But, why?" George insisted. "Why?"

Pheen looked from her brother to her father. A white towel had been wrapped around her sister's neck. Only her face was visible. She hadn't paid attention because all she could think of in the moment was that Nelle was dead, gone from this world forever. She gulped back a sob.

"I pointed it out to Mr. Sloane," her daddy was answering George. "I asked him why anyone would have wrapped a towel around her neck like that. He didn't know, but he said it would take at least four hours to open the casket and as long again to seal it shut. And we'd have to pay for the time and any damage to the casket.

"And for what, George?" John Keller was angry now. "What would we do if, if," he choked on his thoughts and cleared his throat. "If there was evidence of violence done to Nelle, what could I do about it? The police were called there in California."

"We could hire a private investigator!" George cried.

"And how would we pay him? And then what? Arnett is on his way to the Pacific—he's out of reach."

"I hope he's on his way to hell, may God forgive me," Grandma Lavinia stood up slowly. "I'm going to lie down for a while, Nan, then I will help you get supper on the table."

Local War Bride Dies in California! The *Big Sandy* newspaper carried the story of Nelle's accidental gas poisoning in a short write-up in Friday's edition of the paper. Cousin Alpha and her husband Fred were the first to show up on Brushy. They brought a generous portion of a ham.

"What a horrible shame! To lose our Nelle in such a senseless accident!" Alpha hugged Nan hard. "There'll be people coming by. I knew you wouldn't feel like cooking." She took off her coat, underneath she wore an apron over her dress. "You rest, Nan."

"I can't sit," Nan demurred. "I need to be doing something."

Alpha and Fred were only the first of the stream of visitors. Family and close friends, and the minister of their church came to honor the memory of Nelle, to sit with the grieving, to offer food. Others came out of sheer curiosity, avid to hear all the details of Nelle's trip to California, the casket returning so soon after, even to cry false tears over the recent loss of her child. Frank and Harry's girlfriends showed up with Mae. George got up and left the room when he saw Mae and she flinched. Pheen went forward and hugged her.

"I'm so sorry, Pheen," Mae whispered. "People in town are talking about Hobart not coming home for the funeral."

"He's at sea," Pheen acknowledged and looked away. "Maybe it's best he's not here."

"Daddy would've come with me," Mae twisted a handkerchief between her fingers, "but Mama's feeling poorly and Lizzie's not very good at looking after the sick." The two of them were standing apart from the others in the living room. Mae gulped. "There's something you should know, Pheen." She glanced about to make sure no one could overhear their conversation. "Mama's had a letter from Hobart. He…he said he didn't want to think it, but that Nelle had been very quiet and depressed all the time she was there in California."

"No!" Pheen hissed, shaking her head before Mae could finish. "No!"

Mae grasped Pheen's arm as she turned away. "I didn't say I believed it! Nelle would never! Never!" Mae heaved a sigh. "But you know Lizzie. She's purely hateful about Nelle, always has been. I just wanted you to know, if you hear anything like that, I don't believe a word of it."

The funeral was held a week later, when Nelle was laid to rest beside her infant daughter. A simple stone plaque marked her resting place with her name. *Elanor Rose Arnett.* Pheen wanted to take a chisel to the stone, to make it read *Elanor Rose Keller.* If she'd stayed a Keller, maybe she'd still be with them. But then, the dull thought came to her that Nelle had chosen to marry Hobart, had been determined to be with him in California. She turned away from the grave and followed her family back down the ridgetop to home.

The weeks and months which followed did nothing to ease the ache in her heart. Pheen did her schoolwork, did her chores, let the war news wash over her. When September rolled around and George turned eighteen, his daddy drove him to Louisa to enlist in the Army and to have a beer man-to-man with his son.

"I just need to get out of here," George confided to Pheen. "I'm sick of people whispering about Nelle." He'd heard the rumors, too. "And," he added, his face grim, "I'm going to do my part to end this damned war. When it's over, and Hobart Arnett comes home, I'll beat the truth out of him."

The war ended and George came home from Europe. Harry came home as well, but Frank remained, buried in the cemetery at Dunkirk. Hobart didn't show his face on Brushy, someone said he'd stayed in the service. Pheen didn't care where he was. It was enough that she'd never have to see him again. In the spring of 1948, Harry and his wife Susie came to Pheen with a suggestion.

Harry sat on the front porch steps, talking with Lewis. Susie held her year-old son, asleep in her arms, and sat in the swing with Pheen.

"Harry and me, we're moving up north, to Ohio." She laughed. "Way up north—all the way to Sandusky on Lake Erie. Harry's already got a steady job lined up at the American Crayon Company." She adjusted her son as he nestled closer to her. "Why don't you come with us? I'm sure you can find work, and it'd be nice to have some company while I'm home with little Frank."

Susie stopped the motion of the swing and looked directly at Pheen.

"If you get too homesick, you can always move back. You aren't seeing anybody here, are you?"

"No, no one." Pheen stared at her hands. She didn't go anywhere to meet anyone, mostly she even avoided church these days.

"I thought not. You need a fresh start, like Harry." She glanced at her husband and lowered her voice. "Being back home, there's just too many reminders of his brother. It's been hard on him."

And without much thought, Pheen jumped at the offer. She packed her clothes, hugged her parents and Grandma Lavinia good-bye, promised Virgie and Lewis she'd write, and last of all, packed the photograph of Nelle her parents had taken when she was sixteen and still in school. The portrait showed her strong face, a hint of a smile, a hint of her strength and stubbornness. It was like taking her sister with her into the unknown. And maybe, just maybe, the dreams would stop. The recurring dream of Nelle, buried in that glass-fronted coffin. Of her sister's eyes opening, of her hands coming up to slowly pull the towel away from her neck.

CHAPTER SIXTEEN
1981

Pheen woke with a start, but the bed beside her was empty. Tommy was always up early these days, the summer months were the busiest for their farm stand. Moretti's sweet corn and melons were in high demand. She turned over on her side, facing the wall—the photograph of Nelle stared back at her. Rubbing her hand across her face, Pheen threw the covers back and sat up, swinging her legs over the edge of the bed. The nightmare had come again, hitting her as hard as it had in the early years of her life in Sandusky.

She'd lived with Harry and Susie on Depot Street, in the bottom half of a duplex Harry had purchased with his wartime savings. A few streets closer to downtown, she'd found work waitressing at a little restaurant and enrolled in adult evening classes at the high school to train as an office assistant. The restaurant did a brisk lunchtime business for folks getting a meal before their evening shift began at any one of a number of local factories. Pheen had worked there for about a year when a new patron began to come in for lunch nearly every day. Tommy Moretti was a dark-haired young man with black eyes and a ready smile—born and raised in Sandusky in a neighborhood of Italian families. He worked second shift in maintenance at the Barr Rubber factory. It took him six weeks to ask her for a date—and six months to ask her to marry him.

They moved into the upstairs half of Harry and Susie's duplex, where they lived until Tommy got hired at the brand new Sandusky Ford plant. By then Pheen was an office receptionist for a local doctor. They bought a house outside of town on a couple of acres, and Tommy started a garden. Their first child came along in 1957, when they'd almost given up hope of a baby. Sarah Rose was followed two years later by John Thomas and their family was complete.

Two-week summer vacations were spent on Brushy with her folks. Tommy's willingness to pitch in with the farm chores made him a hit with John and Nan, and Grandma Lavinia threatened to adopt him. Her kids grew up surrounded by the same love and sense of belonging that Pheen had always known on Brushy. Lewis lived in the old Jordan place with his wife Georgina, three stair-step girls—Nellie, Fanny, and Nancy, and a passel of hound dogs. Virgie—or Ginny as she preferred to be called—had moved to Pikeville, where she and her husband Russ owned a small realty company. They were childless by choice and traveled the states in Russ' Cadillac convertible, spending winters in Florida. George and his wife Mercy lived in Cincinnati, where George had his own car repair shop. Their daughter, Karen Rose, had followed her dad into the shop. George boasted she was a better mechanic than her father. The family was still intact—except for Grandma Lavinia, who'd passed away in her sleep in the mid-sixties, and Nelle—always and forever, Nelle was missing from every milestone of her adult life, Pheen thought.

Getting dressed, Pheen stood for a moment before Nelle's photo.

"I miss you, Nelle," she whispered.

The house was as clean as she could make it—floors mopped, dusting done, bathroom fixtures shining, clean linens on the bed in the spare bedroom and in John's room. The refrigerator was filled with her home-made potato salad, using newly-dug red potatoes from their garden, coleslaw, and sliced muskmelon. Fresh hamburger, buns, onions, condiments. She ran through the preparations for tonight's meal, and for tomorrow's meals. Sarah was coming home from Columbus, if she could get away from her graduate studies long enough. John was off on a fishing trip on the Erie islands. His room was going to house George and Mercy for the night or two that they were here. And the spare room was ready for her mother. Her momma had called two days ago, to say that she was coming to Ohio and that George and Mercy would bring her. Her daddy wasn't up to the journey. She had something she wanted to show Pheen, she said, but she wouldn't divulge what it was over the phone.

"Tommy," George pushed his chair back from the table, "I swear, that's the best sweet corn I've ever eaten! You gonna show Mercy and me that garden of yours?"

"I need to get out and walk around," Mercy chimed in, "after all that traveling today!"

"Say no more," Tommy stood up. "Wait till you see the watermelons Pheen planted. Sugar Babies, they're called."

As the trio went outside, Pheen turned to her mother. "You want anything else? More coffee? I've made a peach cobbler for dessert and a blueberry coffeecake for breakfast." She was aware that she was talking too much, suddenly nervous. George hadn't said a word if he knew why their momma had planned this trip north. "Momma, you're okay, aren't you? No bad news from the doctor? Daddy's heart worse?"

Nan sighed and shook her head. She got up and retrieved her purse from the countertop.

"I've brought a letter I want you to read." She drew a crumpled envelope from her purse. "I won't say no more. Just read it and tell me what you think." She handed it to Pheen and sat down again.

Bewildered, Pheen took the letter from her mother and smoothed out the envelope. It was addressed to her mother. The return address shocked her: *Hobart Arnett, Dog Leg Road, Marysville, Ohio.*

"What on earth?" She raised a puzzled face to her mother.

"Go on, read it," Nan urged.

Pheen pulled out a single sheet of paper, unfolded it, and began to read.

Dear Nancy,

Well, I expect you'll be surprised to get a letter from me after all this time. I hope you and yours are doing good. My sister Mae told me that you all are still living in the old home place on Brushy. The truth of the matter is, I've got the cancer and the doctors don't think I'll live much longer. I'm writing you this from my hospital bed, I don't want Ellen to know. She and I got married a couple of years after I got home from the war and moved up here. We've got us a nice home and two grown kids—a boy and a girl.

Pheen glanced up at her mother. Trust Hobart— bragging about how his life was so good and her sister dead and forgotten. Her hand tightened on the letter.

"Please," Nan implored, "keep reading."

Pheen blew out her breath and focused on the letter once more. Hobart's handwriting was shaky, it was hard to read.

My mind has been drifting back through all the long years since my darling Nelle died. I have never forgotten my beautiful wife. I see her whenever I close my eyes and in my dreams she comes to me as sweet as any man could ever want. I wish with all my heart that I could see her once more, that our last morning together could come again and I could take back everything that happened then. I never meant to lose her, I have always loved that golden-haired little girl of mine. And I pray the good Lord will forgive me and I'll be taken up to heaven where we can be reunited for all eternity.
Your son-in-law, Hobart Arnett

Pheen read through the letter a second time, as Nan waited silently.

"He killed her, didn't he?"

Her mother nodded.

"I believe he did. He's all but come out and said it, hasn't he?"

Pheen nodded.

"Nelle wrote to me, you know," she told her mother. "She said they argued from the time she got to California. He didn't want her there. He tried to browbeat her into going home.

"I think they were fighting that morning. I think he lost his temper and strangled her and the Navy knew it, but they covered up and told the local police a story. Poor

Nelle, depressed over her baby's death, turning the gas on 'by accident.' Then they shipped him out to sea."

She returned the letter to the envelope and handed it to her mother.

"That's what your daddy said. That towel was wrapped around her neck to hide the bruising." Her mother smiled sadly, "Doesn't bring Nelle back, does it?"

No, Pheen thought, it didn't. She'd thought about that glass viewing window in the casket over the years. Someone out there in California had made sure that Nelle's family knew she hadn't killed herself—those glass-viewing windows weren't much in use in caskets when Nelle had died. Whoever it was, they'd made sure that towel was visible, that it set up a doubt about any implication of suicide and the official, accidental cause of death.

Tommy came out of the master bathroom in his pajamas and came to where Pheen sat on the side of the bed, holding Nelle's photo. He joined her, pulling her close in his arms and dropped a kiss on the top of her head.

"Maybe now," he suggested softly, "she's at peace and your nightmares will stop."

Tracing the line of her sister's cheek with her finger, Pheen nodded. She'd known all along that Nelle hadn't killed herself, that Hobart must have been responsible. All these years, he'd had to live with that knowledge, that he'd killed her in a moment of anger and nothing he could do would ever bring her back. But he'd waited until he was dying to face what he'd done, and maybe, she thought, maybe the cancer was the only justice they'd ever get. She set the photo gently on the bedside table.

The last thing she saw as she turned out the light was Nelle's smile, Nelle's eyes staring at her—as if to say, put the grieving away, Pheen. Nelle, she saw now, had been with her every step of the way into her life all these long years after the war. Nelle was here now with her and always would be—the bond they shared—the love between sisters—had not died with Nelle.